The TORCH keepers

THE TORCH KEEPERS

HOSANNA EMILY

Published by S.C. TreeHouse Press
press.sctreehouse.com

The Torch Keepers
Copyright © 2019 by Hosanna Emily
www.havingaheartlikehis.blogspot.com

Cover design: Alea Harper
Illustrations: Caroline Ruth

Published in association with Storytellers a protected series of S.C. TreeHouse LLC and S.C. TreeHouse Press a protected series of S.C. TreeHouse LLC and Hosanna Emily.

S.C.TREEHOUSE PRESS and S.C. TreeHouse Press' logo are registered trademarks of S.C. TreeHouse LLC.

Printed in the United States of America.

ISBN: 978-0-578-56517-0

to the soul thriving with a passion to live for the King:
keep the torch burning;
you're never alone.

TABLE OF CONTENTS

Though your sins are like scarlet,

they shall be as white as snow.

Isaiah 1:18

Prologue

another night, tonight;
another rising cry that is carried away

Always keep the fire burning."

"Why, Mama?" The child's tiny hand reached up to point at the flickering, blue flame. She turned toward her mother, the firelight picking up streaks of gold in her mother's dark hair. "Why must we keep the fire burning?" The girl tilted her head. Her sapphire eyes shone in the pale light.

"Because, my child." The woman knelt and took her daughter's hand in hers. "Because we are the King's Torch Keepers. We must always follow our calling, for it is a noble one."

They worked as one to lift the dying torch down from its elevated place by the city gate, the rough reeds of its handle scratching their fingers. Kneeling, the woman held an unlit torch to the flame and waited for the fire to catch as the end of the wick met old with new.

The former torch's flame grew low in the mother's hand, and the fire blinked several times before fading to blackness. The young torch burst to life as the fire caught, the ever-glowing flames driving the shadows back into the desert wilderness. The flame's steady, blue glow cut through the air as it was lifted high to be a sentinel to those beyond the city's walls.

"One day, my child, you will be the Torch Keeper." The woman stared out into the still night. "And then you too will hold this great responsibility to keep the flame alive. The loyalty of the city will be in your hands."

The child nodded. Her bright smile flashed a dimple in her cheek. "I will, Mama. I'll never let it die."

The woman lifted her daughter into her arms and pressed soft kisses against the little girl's curly hair as they slipped through the city gates. Once behind the barricades, she tucked the child into a low bed under the eaves of a thatched roof. Their eyes met, blue against brown. The girl smiled.

A man with the same tan complexion joined the woman, and they looked down on the girl, their faces worn from the harsh, desert wind. Holding her daughter's hand, the mother knelt at the bedside to push away a lock of midnight hair from the child's forehead.

"It's not an easy job." Her whisper broke through cracked lips. "But you must be strong. The kingdom of Érkeos is counting on you, my child."

1

ka-ꝺaꝛa

golden rays,
a calling embrace

Do I look pretty, Ka-Mama?" I lifted my cheeks to the mirror and brushed back the curls that tickled my face. Now I could see my eyes, blue just like Daddy's. Grinning, I pushed my hands down, rubbing my sparkly dress. "I like this new outfit you made me."

"One more thing, and then I'll have a look at you, my little Ka -Dara." My mama pulled back my hair with a ribbon and then took me in her arms. I saw her necklace sparkle, and I pulled away slightly.

"Can I try it on?" I breathed.

She slipped the necklace around my own neck, and I sighed, deep. When Ka-Mama put it back on herself, I stared into her dark eyes. My face grew warm. "You're beautiful too, Ka-Mama. I'm so happy we're gonna have a celebra–, cele–, what's it called again?"

"A celebration?" She laughed. "Tonight we will celebrate the anniversary of our nation's birth."

My mouth opened wide. "Oh, I 'member! That was when the King made our land and the first two people in it! They were Torch Keepers to protect us against bad guys. Like you and Ka-Daddy do!"

"Yes," she said and touched the end of my nose, "and one day you, my child."

My smile went away as I turned back to look at my reflection. I pulled my bottom lip in and wrinkled my forehead. "My teacher said, 'today is an epoch in our time.' I don't know what that means, but he told us that some people say the moon will pop up in the sky when the sun goes down. I hope it does, 'cause I never saw the moon before. What does it look like, Ka-Mama?"

She shook her head. "None of us knows, save the King. The moon hasn't risen since the beginning of time."

"I think it's pink." I ran to the window to stare into the sky. "But my teacher said that those super wise people who study the stars say the moon might be orange or yellow. They're probably right, 'cause they're smarter than me."

"Ka-Dara." She took my hand and squeezed it tight. "We must not believe everything others say. Even learned people are often wrong."

"What about you and Ka-Daddy?" My lips turned downward. I fiddled with the necklace she wore, but she gently uncurled my fingers.

She laughed. "We're wrong too sometimes."

14

The wooden door swung open, and the sounds and smells of the party filled the air. I squealed and ran forward, throwing myself against Ka-Daddy's legs.

"I knew you'd be home soon! Did you bring me a present? 'Member, you said you would?" My eyes opened wide as I clapped my hands.

"Yes, my princess." He leaned down to give me a hug. When his whiskers tickled my face, I fell over with giggles. I pulled away from the smell of his shirt—my mama called it leather—and saw his eyes look over my head to where Ka-Mama stood. He nodded.

"The rumors? They're that bad?" Ka-Mama walked towards us and touched his shoulder.

His jaw tightened. "With the celebration tonight, we need to be careful. They're always looking for opportunities."

"My present?" I interrupted them and jumped up and down, grabbing my daddy's arms.

"Two," he said. My feet touched the ground as he reached into a rawhide pouch and closed his fist tight. Smile lines lay around his eyes as he held out both fists together. "Which one?"

I bit my lip and rocked from foot to foot. My eyes turned from one hand to the other. Finally, my finger pressed into his left fist. "This one."

He opened his hand. There was nothing.

"You tricked me!" I laughed, grabbing the other fist and trying to pull open his fingers.

He laughed too and quickly opened his fist, putting something on my hand. A bright red fruit! I squealed. Grabbing its squishy skin, I pressed it to my nose and inhaled the sugar-smell. "Oh, it smells *so* good! I'll share it with you, Ka-Daddy. But I need to peel it first." My legs slipped down in a crossed-legged position as I carefully tore away the thin peels. Breaking the juicy insides into three pieces, I handed one to Ka-Daddy, the other to Ka-Mama, and kept the last in my own palm. "One for each of us!"

Ka-Mama took the slice, and we both let the sticky flavors tickle our tongues. It dripped on my chin. When I wiped the juice on my sleeve, Ka-Mama smiled, but her eyes were wet.

"What's wrong, Ka-Mama?" My eyebrows pulled tight, and I jumped back to my feet. "I could give you another piece of my fruit. Do you want it?"

She turned away, placing a hand against her fat tummy. Her gaze met Ka-Daddy's, and his eyebrows pulled together.

"Did you forget my other gift?" Ka-Daddy asked, making me look back at him. He took out a thin, dark bottle and held it in his fingertips.

I pulled away and wrinkled my nose. "What's that?"

"The juice from the moon-flower." His voice lowered. "It's very rare, and you must tell no one of it. Tonight for the celebration, your mother will put a drop in each one of your eyes."

"My eyes? Why?" I jerked to my mother's side and put my hand in hers. "I don't want you to."

"My dear," she said, "your eyes are beautiful like your daddy's. The King gave you bright blue eyes, unlike any other child, for you are set apart to be a Torch Keeper. But the King's

16

enemies will seek you out because of it. This will keep you safe."
She touched my chin and raised it so that I looked in her face.
"You must be brave and trust us."

I stuck out my lower lip. "But why don't you do the drops in
your and Ka-Daddy's eyes too?"

She played with my hair. "My princess, I am a Torch Keeper
by marriage, thus my eyes are not like yours. And your father is
not a child; it's his own decision to make." Ka-Mama and Ka-
Daddy both smiled down on me. "But we need you to be safe."

"I—I'll try to be brave," I said, swallowing hard. "If you want
to, I'm ready for you to put it in."

Ka-Mama's arms surrounded me, warm. She lifted me to my
bed and took the dark bottle between her fingers. My chest
tightened as she hesitated.

"Ka-Mama?" The word trembled on my tongue.

She pressed a kiss against my cheek and raised the bottle. My
eyes stared up at the ceiling. In Ka-Mama's hands, a brown drop
hesitated on the end of the bottle's tip. And fell. Down, down.

Everything grew fuzzy. I jerked away and pulled in a sharp
breath of air. My teeth clenched tight as the second drop
followed. They burned, and I tried not to cry.

"Now, child, come see in the mirror." Ka-Daddy lifted me to
my feet, and I took quiet steps toward my reflection as my vision
returned. The colors around me were like balls of cotton, all
fuzzy. I blinked several times as my hands reached for the mirror,
and I raised my gaze.

A gasp caught in my throat. The girl staring back at my face wasn't me. She wasn't the same girl who laughed earlier, excited for tonight's party. My blue eyes had changed to an ugly brown. The pink color left my cheeks.

My mama sniffed and turned away, wiping her face with the edge of her sleeve.

"It's okay, Ka-Mama," I said. Tears caught in my eyes. Deep breath. "I do like brown almost as much as blue."

"Sometimes we must do hard things, but the King will give us strength." Ka-Daddy pressed me close to his chest. "You are brave, my princess."

"I love you, Ka-Daddy." I stared into his own sky-blue eyes just like mine—but mine weren't anymore. I quickly looked away.

"And I, you." He pushed me back and played with the ends of my curly hair. "But while I was out, I heard Am-Othniel was looking for you. He's in the dancehall tuning the instruments for the celebration. Go have fun with your little friends, my dear."

"Be back before the dance, Ka-Dara!" My mama said as I ran to the door.

"I will." I grinned. "I want Ka-Daddy to have my first dance." I paused and ran back to throw my arms around my mother's tummy which was getting bigger every day. Ka-Daddy said she wasn't fat, but I couldn't put my arms around her anymore. That meant she was at least a tiny bit fat, I think. I let my lips touch Ka-Mama's tummy in a whisper. "Goodbye, baby."

The outside air embraced me in its dry heat as I slipped onto the dusty street. Music rose from where lots of strangers set up for the celebrations. The smells of bread, fruits, and meats cooking on sticks over fires made me smile. Soon, we would feast! I turned toward the streets and left behind my family's house that guarded the city gates.

Behind the wooden walls, the torch flickered with a strong, blue light. And farther in the horizon, dust rose up in clouds as caravans journeyed through the wasteland on their own missions.

2

ka-ðaRa

dance and laughter past,
a new memory today

h ard, white stone touched my feet. Footsteps made funny, deep
sounds against the tall ceilings of the dancehall as I hurried past
big blankets hanging on the walls. Ka-Mama called them
tapestries, but to me they just looked like pretty quilts. The reds
and yellows told stories of the way of the King and the creation of
Érkeos, swept up in the giant blankets. I stopped near one and let
the cloth rub against my fingers. It felt slippery like the new dress
I wore.

I looked up. There was a picture in this blanket, two angry
people running away from a big garden. There was a torch too,
big and blue, like a huge wall of fire. I gasped—the people were
Torch Keepers like my mama and daddy! But somehow, their
eyes were different. They were green and blue at the same time. I
chewed on my lip.

A sound made me turn away. A quiet musical note filled the air and slid around me like lazy clouds in the sky. Tingling ran down my arms as I hurried to the end of the hall where large instruments stood, waiting for use. When night came, the sparkling floors would have a whole bunch of dancing feet while songs filled the air. It would be so fun!

The note faded, and another began, this one higher yet with a smooth feel that surrounded me like a hug. My feet climbed up the stone steps. I reached out and touched the edge of one of the smaller instruments. The glass piece made goosebumps crawl up my arms.

"Oth?" I smiled at my friend as he bent over the instrument with his eyes pressed shut. He shook his head and reached forward to press a key. The music repeated in another note.

When he opened his eyes again, he adjusted a knobby thing and turned toward me. "It's almost perfect, but the note's a bit flat. I need to get it perfect for when I play tonight."

I held my breath as he fiddled with the knobs before pressing the notes. Between the keys, he whispered to me.

"These are hammers; they're soft, covered with the silk of taffworms. When the hammers strike those bronze strings," he said, pointing, "they make vibrations. That's the sound we hear. But if the vibrations are only slightly off—," Am-Othniel pressed a key, and his lips twisted.

His words made no sense, so I looked closely at the glass instrument. Keys stained different shades of gold and brown all lined up at the front of the instrument. Behind them, I could see through the glass frame and into the deeper part of the instrument where dark strings stretched out in all different sizes. When the keys were pushed, the strings in the back wiggled like worms! Am-Othniel leaned his ear near the last string, played it several times, and then stepped back with a grin. I giggled.

He rubbed his hand across the keys. "This is my favorite instrument, the laude-chorda. It's small, but when I play it the music will sing louder than every other sound. It's like standing by a door when wind blows up a fierce sandstorm. It's all you can hear—music."

"Can you play me a song?" I reached forward to press a note, but he grabbed my arm.

"Not 'til the dance tonight. It must be perfectly in tune. If only one instrument is sharp or flat, it will ruin all the others." He motioned to the big jumble of instruments behind him.

I turned in a full circle to examine the instruments with strings, with banging drum-things, and some with twisty tunnels for people to blow through. When I turned back to him, my voice dropped to a whisper. "Can you play all of them?"

"Of course." He shrugged and winked at me. "Just not at the same time."

I giggled. "You should be a minstrel when you grow up. I'd sing with you. You could travel everywhere and play songs to make people dance!"

"I wish my mom thought so." He looked down at the laude-chorda and shook his head. "'Cause Am-Dad was never with us, he can't teach me a trade. Am-Mom said I should learn to be a builder. I guess that's more important than music; people always need builders."

"But if you performed, maybe one day the King would invite you to his palace, and you could perform for him and his great generals. Then your mother would see how good you play!"

He laughed and shrugged it off. "We don't all believe in the King like you do, Ka-Dara." A frown crossed his face as he stared at me. "Hey, what's up with your eyes today?"

"There you are!" The door at the end of the dancehall crashed open to the figure of a girl with bright red hair. "I thought you'd be here, but you could have at least told us!"

"Oh, Ir-Ivah! I was wondering where you were." I rushed down the steps and across the stone floor. In the middle of the room, my friend grabbed me in a tight hug.

She nodded. "And Ir-Haran. I brought him too. He said he wasn't going to the dance tonight, but I just told him he had to, so there." Ir-Ivah grinned and pointed to her short, freckle-faced brother who stood apart and shook hands with Am-Othniel. Boyish grins crossed their faces as they joined our side.

"I don't wanna dance," Ir-Haran mumbled. His eyes crept up to my face, and pinkness rushed to his cheeks. It looked kinda weird. "But if you want me to…"

Ir-Ivah burst in and grabbed my hand. "He'll stand by the dinner tables all night, I'm sure. Oh, but I can't wait for tonight. Ka-Dara, did you hear our teacher say the moon might appear? I wonder what it'll be like!"

"My mom says the moon's just a myth," Am-Othniel said. "Don't set your hopes on it."

"I already have!" Ir-Ivah declared. "And if it doesn't appear, I'll simply die from dashed hopes."

"She says that all the time." Ir-Haran whispered to me, and I hid a laugh behind my hand.

"Do not. I heard what you said, and you're making it all up!" she said and turned to me. "Oh, that ribbon in your hair is so pretty. Did you put it in?"

I giggled. "No, Ka-Mama did."

"Really? I hate when people touch my hair! My own mother would never, ever, ever, ever…"

Am-Othniel raised his hands. "Don't you guys have to take care of everyone's animals? I should finish tuning the instruments, and the sun's already setting."

Ir-Ivah gasped. "I forgot. What did Ir-Dad say about mucking out the stalls, Ir-Haran? What did he say?" She pulled her brother toward the doors but hesitated before touching the cold, stone handles. Ir-Ivah pushed back her red hair and raised her eyes to Am-Othniel's face. "You will promise me the first dance, right? I'll be waiting!"

The doors slammed closed, echoing against the tall ceilings. The pretty blankets that hung high on the walls shivered. It made them look alive. I laughed and turned to Am-Othniel. "First dance to Ir-Ivah?"

He shook his head, and his face wrinkled. "I'll make her music while *she* dances. Last time, she trampled on every one of my toes." He joined in my laughter before hurrying back to the tall stage. Resting his hand on the edge of the instrument, he grinned at me. "Wanna hear a secret?"

I nodded and pulled close to his side.

"We got this laude-chorda yesterday, and I just finished my first tuning. Every time I tune an instrument for the first time, I leave my musician's mark."

"How?" I touched the glass. My finger left a smear, and I wiped it off before Oth saw.

He pulled out a slip of paper and a pen. "See, I can write a note here and slip it between the keys. There's this little area underneath where only a tuner can find it. If anyone tunes it again, they can read what I wrote."

My mouth dropped open. "What are you going to write?"

The pen hesitated on the paper before sweeping across in large, curly letters. When he was done, Am-Othniel blew and handed it to me.

I read it slowly. "'Don't let anyone steal your music. AO.' What does AO mean?"

His forehead wrinkled. "I think those are my initials. Like the A is my first name, and the O is for Othniel. That's what Am-Mom told me."

"Oh, but how could someone steal your music?" I ran a hand through my curly hair. "I mean, no one can take your hands and play your music for you. Why'd you write that? That's silly."

He frowned. "I don't know. It was just the message I felt." Am-Othniel shrugged before folding the paper in half. It hesitated on the edge of the instrument. My arms tensed as he let go of the secret note to slip between the keys and into the dark bottom of the laude-chorda where the glass was deep brown.

I looked at the instruments and turned to face the long dancehall. "I can't wait for tonight."

"Me neither." He turned to look at his work. "But I have a woodwind to examine and make sure it's ready. Then the party can begin."

"I would skip the dancing and sing with you, but I promised Ka-Daddy my first dance. If you want to have a turn dancing, I won't step on your toes." My fingers rested on his.

"I'd like that."

The door swung open again, and I turned toward the orange light that flew into the room. A smile broke across my face. "Ka-Mama?"

"Come, child." She commanded in a low tone. "We must go quickly."

I hurried forward and grabbed her hand. "But what about Oth? Does he need to come too?"

Wrinkles lined Ka-Mama's forehead. She turned to Oth who stood still by the instruments all lined up. "Child, if you ever believe in the way of the King, now is the time."

He stared at Ka-Mama. "What?"

She took me in her arms and shook her head slowly. "I don't think there will be a celebration tonight. Am-Othniel, you must run to your mother and pray that help comes."

My feet left the ground as my mama swept me away in the busy streets. We stumbled, running around people, and I grabbed Ka-Mama's necklace in one hand. My head twisted back to stare at the open dancehall where my friend stood among the stone floors and silky blankets on the walls. I saw the picture of the two Torch Keepers and the big fire. And then it was gone. Noisy people cut off my vision. I grabbed my mother's arms as shoppers and sellers yelled out prices. The same yummy smells made my tummy growl, but I stared above the city walls.

Most people saw the orange of the setting sun in the sky far away. But further beyond, a strange cloud grew.

As the first stars began to shine, a thick green haze seemed to rise. I rubbed my eyes as if in a dream, but the color only became stronger.

The cabin door swung shut behind me. My feet touched the ground, and I looked in my mother's eyes. My lips trembled.

"Now is the time to be brave, my princess." Ka-Mama pushed aside a stray curl and grasped my hand in her cold one. "We must flee."

3

Rekém

strength on air
fading to mist

You're gonna be proud of me. I'll show you!" I said, clenching my hands together as I faced Teion. My older brother snorted.

"Ha, as if you could do something brave, Rekém. Do something big, and we'll see." His voice hissed in the twilight glow as he turned away from me, muttering under his breath. "I could win this entire battle by myself. I could conquer the desert and liberate every city. And one day I will."

"I know you will; you're the Prince, Teion! That's way bigger than anything I could ever be."

"It's not enough. I can do more, be more!" He slammed two fists together. "I'll be more than just a prince. I'll be the strongest, bravest leader there ever was, second in command to no one, not even the silly, old King. I'll be the only ruler of Érkeos, a legend for ages to come." Teion laughed. "But you, you're just a child.

This is your chance to do something—an entire aviation force at your disposal. Ha! Let's hope you don't fail miserably."

My eyes fell. "Then maybe I shouldn't try."

Teion twisted his lips into a sharp grin. "Don't be a fool, little brother. Just do your job and let no one escape." He paused and knelt to my side. Our shoulders pressed together as he pointed into the desert. "There's a city out there," he whispered, "a city waiting to be liberated. This isn't just a war. This is a fight for freedom, to deliver these people from the King's bondage. When I rule, they'll be free."

I glanced at my brother. For a moment, his hand rested, nearly around me. Light reflected on his jaw, strong like the Prince he was. My chest swelled.

Teion jerked to his feet. "Fight hard. You know what happens if you fail me." He gave a smirk and disappeared into the murky light.

"I won't!" I yelled after him. "I'll do everything you said!"

He never turned around.

Shadows began to crawl across the desert as I released my breath. Brushing a hand through my hair, I stared at the first stars beginning to shine. They shot from one side of the sky to the other then curled in circled movements. The stars danced as if celebrating our upcoming victory. My eyes dropped lower. The horizon faded to grey as my eyes traced the skyline.

My fist tightened around the bow that was slung over my shoulder. A quiver of arrows cut into the small of my back, but I held my chin up. The razor-sharp arrowheads were ready, their shafts filled with powder that would explode on impact. This battle was *real.* And I was a part of it.

Pushing my shoulders back, I marched toward the awaiting army. My gaze never left the horizon as I remembered my commands.

The first shadows of blackness would come. Then we would ride. We would ride like phantoms in the shadows that were never seen until they struck the final blow.

The silhouettes of my fellow warriors shifted from foot to foot in the still-hot sand. They reached for the scaly necks of their mounts. The flame-wings lowered to the ground, pulling their leathery wings tight to their bodies. The beasts lay, only black shadows, but in the battle that would change. They would glow green like lightning for our armies.

I found my own flame-wing and slipped onto the hot back that scratched my legs. The beast let out a hiss as his body tensed.

"There," I whispered to the winged creature. I pointed ahead to where a city glowed pale blue, only a speck in the desert world. "There is our mission. We can't fail Teion." I let out a deep breath and grinned. "This is so cool."

The flame-wing sank his claws into the ground. His golden eyes turned toward me and then back to the sky as if testing for readiness. My gaze followed. Every muscle in my body seemed to burst into fire as the darkness embraced the earth.

"Riders, mount for your Prince!" I spoke the words I had heard Teion's voice boom so many times. But my speech came out squeaky and high. I swallowed hard.

Together, the band of followers grasped their flame-wings and secured bows and quivers upon their backs. Every eye watched me for the final command.

I eyed the cohort. My breath caught as two dozen riders met my gaze. The trained warriors were the ones small enough to fly on the wind, but their hard faces told stories of courage. We would ride to victory or our deaths for the same noble cause.

I turned back to my flame-wing. My arms quivered. I wasn't old enough, strong enough, brave enough to lead so many warriors. How could a boy lead an army? But taking a deep breath, I whispered to my flame-wing, and then released the cry. "For the Prince!"

The flame-wing threw itself forward. In an instant, my body froze from a blast of cold air. Wind shot through my hair and cut my face, but my fingers only grasped tighter onto a leather strap around my mount's neck. By my side, the creature raised long, thick wings and began to soar on the edge of the sky.

I turned to stare behind me, but the other riders had disappeared into the night. My heart tightened in my chest. Alone with my mount, the icy wind seemed to grasp at my throat and squeeze tight. I sucked in air between my teeth. The flame-wing glided silently, and I scanned the horizon. But it was empty. Already the city was far below us, a tiny sapphire jewel in the black world.

Yet out of the blackness, another light shone. A war cry sounded. Shadows turned into a hundred warriors as the armies besieged the city on desert ground. Flames of green torches shone against the blue city, two forces clashing.

I shivered, but it turned into a grin. This was just like a game, but now I was part of it.

The mount beneath me lowered to the war zone. Individual attackers began to take shape as they crashed through the front gates and threw themselves into the city. The attack hesitated when defenders rushed to the city walls. The first cries of death broke through the night, and I took it in with an awestruck gasp.

And then my eyes froze. On the other end of the city, a handful of figures broke away from the wall. They tried to escape through the desert, only a pale blue torch lighting their way.

My flame-wing leapt in the wind, bursting to life as it shot in the direction of our prey. Its wings began to burn a brilliant green as it dove low to the ground.

I grabbed my bow. Clenching my teeth together, I fitted an arrow against the string. I pulled back. The feather brushed my cheek, and I hesitated.

We burst forward with the flame-wing's sweeping, green glow. And as our wind touched the escaping citizens, my arrow sliced into the ground at their feet.

It hit dirt. As my mount turned full upward into the air, we left behind a loud explosion. I strained my neck to see the earth once more, but all that was left of the enemy was a smoky glare.

"That was huge!" I clasped my hands together. I lunged back and nearly fell off the flame-wing, hurrying to grab onto it again. But I could feel my chest expanding with warmth as we soared in the wind. We were brave. We were heroes.

Another explosion sounded nearby as a rider fired an arrow, destroying the victims. With excitement tensing my arms, I edged my flame-wing back toward the ground where our next prey waited. Every arrow exploded like a volcano as warriors flew by on their emerald-winged beasts. No one could stop us. It was a game we played, seeing how many shadowy figures we could blow up before dawn arrived. They were the enemy, after all.

As we climbed in the air after another victory, I steered my mount back toward the city. Already, green flames were clapping their hands above the city walls, and the number of escapees lessened. At the gates, I slipped onto the now-cold sand. The flame-wing crouched and waited as I marched forward. Bodies lay before the city walls, but they were only shadows I stepped around. At the gates, I stopped and let my heart grow hot in our victory.

The gates were broken and cut. Behind them, the sounds of screaming grew silent under the smell of burning rubble. But I turned my chin up toward the great entrance of the city that had once been so proud. Strange writing was etched above the gates, and I twisted my lips trying to discern the weird letters. They were secret pictures, invisible meanings.

A torch stood tall in the sand, flickering light against the protruding night. Its thick, green color circled around me. It was the last remnant of life outside the gates, a serpent waiting, ready to launch at our enemy and cut them with burning fangs. The city was ours now.

I bowed my head toward the flame and entered the city. A victorious cheer burned in my chest. Our mission was complete.

"Well done, young warrior. You've proved yourself." A man dressed in black swept towards me from the city square. I recognized him as one of the Liberation's leaders, and his eyes shone in the green light as he clasped a hand against my shoulder. "You have the makings of a general like your brother."

Several other warriors nodded and joined the procession back to camp, leaving behind the smoking remnants of the city. I ran in front of them and clambered onto my flame-wing, raising my bow in the air and cheering for the heroic veterans.

And then I caught my brother's eye. Teion stared at me, shook his head, and turned back into the city. My smile faded.

4

ka-ðara

for the enduring promises shine,
stars in darkness

Ka-Mama, I'm scared." I threw my arms tight around her neck and hid my face as we snuck through the streets. "I want Ka-Daddy. Where is he?"

"Ka-Daddy is at the city gate, my princess. We must be brave for him."

A groan cut the air as she reached for a tall door. She stiffened as we slipped inside the shadows. The scent of fresh hay mixed with sweaty animal fur surrounded us.

My eyebrows shot up. "Are we gonna see Ir-Ivah and Ir-Haran? They take care of the animals. I wanna see them so I won't be scared anymore."

"No, child. They are not here. We must be quiet." She placed a finger on my lips before slipping me down onto the hay. Sharp pieces poked my feet.

Blinking lights slipped through the cracks in the wooden stable. I frowned as the shadows danced. Blackness gave way to flashes of blue and then green, but the colors faded again into night. I bit my cheek as I scanned the room, but my eyes lit up when my mother opened a stall.

"Oh, can we ride one? I always wanted to!" I rushed to the stall and froze when an animal lowered its nose to sniff my hair. I swallowed down a cry and grabbed onto Ka-Mama's leg.

"Shh." Ka-Mama reached for my hand and lifted it to the animal's nose. The deer gave a snort and tossed his head, waving sharp, twisty horns. I screamed and buried myself in my mother's arms.

"Be brave; he will not harm you. The sabbax deer act fierce, but they are calm and gentle." Ka-Mama barely whispered the words through her tight lips as she put a rope around the deer's neck. The animal grew quiet and followed her as she stepped into the main part of the stable.

I forced myself to squint up at the deer. Tall, knobby legs met a strong body that was dark gold in the dim light. A tail shook back and forth when my mother rubbed the animal's nose.

"We must go, my dear." She gave me a tight squeeze. Slipping me onto the sabbax deer's back, Ka-Mama led us back into the night air. I grabbed the rope. The animal's fur brushed my legs, warm and soft.

Some thick, smoky air made me cough, and I swung my head around to stare at the center of the city. The dancehall glowed in strange colors of green as huge poofs of smoke poured out and stained the air. My eyes grew wide.

"Ka-Mama! There's fire!"

"Quiet."

My mother quickened to a jog as we ran through empty streets. I squeezed the deer with my legs and let my hands grab its fur as we bumped up and down. The screaming and the crackling fire made my body stiffen, and I tried to raise my shoulders to cover my ears. Every muscle in my body hurt.

A dark wall rose above us. My eyebrows lowered, and I leaned forward to hiss to my mother. "Where's the gate? What are we doing here?"

She didn't respond. Instead, she knelt and seemed to push something. Out of the darkness, the wall opened into a narrow trapdoor. The desert waited before us like an empty blanket.

As soon as the desert air met us, Ka-Mama joined my side. "Now we ride." She took a deep breath and hoisted herself onto the animal. I leaned back into my mother and patted her tummy.

"You and me and baby. When will Ka-Daddy come?"

The deer jumped forward, and I grasped for its neck. When the rocky ground of the city's edge changed to thick sand, his hooves pressed forward. Air rubbed my face, and the ground galloped by. The city lights grew smaller behind us as the deer ran super-fast into the night.

But as soon as I let my shoulders relax, color caught my eye. Something to my left burst into light. A whooshing sound swept through the air, but it grew louder as the earth exploded around us.

"Ka-Mama!" I screamed. My body jerked back against hers. I threw up my hands to guard against the sand that burned my eyes.

My mama's arms grew tight around me, and the sabbax burst to a full run.

Other flashes of light followed by explosions erupted in the darkness, but I buried myself in Ka-Mama's chest and hid from them all. Tears cut my cheeks as my body shook. We rode super fast. The animal kept on running, air pressed against us, and finally the world grew silent.

I opened my eyes. Wiping my cheeks with sandy palms, I stared into the darkness. Dust splashed onto my legs, and cold air made my hair billow away from my face. Then everything grew calm except for the continual sweeping of the sabbax's legs.

My gaze turned up. I looked at the silent black sky and eyed the handful of stars that glared down upon me. But no moon rose. The celebration, the excitement, it had all been nothing. Only darkness was here.

I said nothing. My lips pressed closed, and I held tight to the deer's soft back. We ran forward into emptiness.

When black faded to a pale grey, I blinked. The desert's fingers let go, and a mountain rose out of the earth. Yellow sand gave way to rocks, and some scratchy bushes lined a path that rose high before us.

But this mountain wasn't the only one in the desert. Behind the first hills peeked a whole row of mountains and valleys. Their colors grew from green to blue to purple as they spread farther than I could see. My mouth dropped open, and I wanted to reach out and touch the farthest one, to see how sand could tower up so high in the air.

Then my mouth grew dry. People said there were volcanoes in the mountains. What if one exploded and burned me? I grabbed the deer tighter.

Our mount slowed back to a trot as his legs arched against the smooth rocks. Each step rocked me like when I had sat on my daddy's lap. He would shake me until I burst into giggles, and then we would fall backwards in each other's arms and stare at the stars as they danced, seeing how many we could count. "There's even more," he would say, "and the King has named every one of them."

"Ka-Mama," I said, "When will Ka-Daddy come with us?"

She shook her head. "He is fighting for the way of the King. We must accept the King's will."

I chewed on my cheek. "What does that mean?"

Ka-Mama didn't answer. She pulled the animal still and grunted as she pushed herself off its slender back. I giggled and crawled into Ka-Mama's arms, patting the deer's soft fur.

"You're nice. I like you."

My mama tied the deer to a brambly brush. The animal's sides rose and fell with quick breathing as we left it and hurried up the mountain. Shadows fell around us as stones crunched under our feet. I slipped on smooth pebbles but grabbed Ka-Mama's hand as we climbed forward. Some rocks got in my shoes and hurt my feet.

The sandy world changed to rock with edges of moss. A shivering statue rose with one big, grey-brown leg and green leafy things like hair on the top. I stared at it.

"Is it a cactus? It looks so squiggly." I traced it against the sky with my finger.

Ka-Mama laughed. "It's a tree. Here, the land is very different. You will learn to love it, my child."

My eyes opened wide. "We will live here?" I asked. "You and me and Ka-Daddy and the baby? When will my friends come? Oh look—is this our home?"

City walls towered from the rocky ground as if they were built of the same stone they stood on. A blue light shone from the torch near the city gate, and weird but pretty writing swept above the gate like a welcome sign. I paused to read it, but my mother pulled me close to her side.

We went faster as we avoided the gates and crept by the side of the city. As she had done before, Ka-Mama paused by the side of the wall and pushed part of it inward. A secret door swung open.

I held tight to my mama's dress as we trotted through the sleeping city. The sun already shone on the cobblestones we stepped on. And then I smelled flowers.

Ka-Mama paused. I raised my eyes, and my mouth dropped open in a smile. I raced forward and toward a white arch. Bushes and vines swept around the arch and on both sides, filling the world with lots of cute flowers.

"See, Ka-Mama?" I picked a flower from the bush, giving it to her with a giggle. "It's so pretty! Is pink your favorite color?"

Her brown eyes filled with tears. She picked me up and squeezed tight. "Yes, it is. But I love you much more than flowers."

I pulled away and placed my hands on her wet cheeks. "Don't cry, Ka-Mama."

Light sparkled on her tanned face as if the sun smiled upon her. She knelt to my height as she placed my feet back onto the ground. Ka-Mama tucked the flower behind my ear.

"Ka-Dara," she said, "don't forget how much I love you. I will be gone for a little while, but don't be afraid. You are strong, my princess."

"But why, Ka-Mama?"

She nudged me toward the archway. "Sit here by the flowers. These people are kind, and they will take care of you. I will return, if the King wills. Be brave. I love you, my child."

She slipped something around my neck. And then she was gone.

"No, Ka-Mama!" I jumped to my feet and screamed at the alley where she had disappeared. "Ka-Mama, wait! I want to go with you! I want to go home! I want Ka-Daddy!"

Tears blinded my vision as I stumbled forward. The flower slipped from my ear and fell, trampled upon the ground. I tripped and stumbled against the stones. It cut my legs and my new dress. Blood stained the ground's rough edges. But I raised my eyes to stare down the alley as I tried to push myself up and find the one who had left me. I felt my mama's necklace around my throat, but it felt like it would choke me.

"Ka-Mama!" My voice cracked, and I sank back onto the rocks. "Ka-Mama, I need you."

But there was no response. The sun rose on the pink blossoms that filled the air with perfume, but I waited to hear my mama's voice. It never came.

5

Rekém

*in twilight, he stumbles
and can't go back*

Wasn't it awesome?" I screamed to Teion over the hiss of the wind. The flame-wing I flew on turned his head quickly but straightened and continued his flight across the desert's carpet.

Teion glanced at me. Dark hair crept over his eyes, but the wind threw it back behind his ear. His jawbone tensed, and he ignored my comment.

I leaned forward as the desert swept below us. Our Liberation camp had long since disappeared, but home would soon be on the horizon. Sand faded to rocky ground, from gold to grey.

Cold air blasted my face, and I inhaled it deeply. The scent of the Sea made my arms tense. A grin crept onto my face.

As we flew, spots of green appeared like ants rushing towards us. They began to solidify to trees, forests, and then the world exploded into blueness.

Beyond the band of trees, the Sea swept farther than my eyes could see. It seemed to go on forever, like a blue blanket covering the never-ending ground.

I dug my heels in the flame-wing's side. He dove downward. A million pins seemed to prick my arms at once as we let gravity take us back to earth. My stomach lurched, but I swallowed hard. Leaning close to the beast's neck, we flew as one.

The ground rushed to meet us. A second before we hit, the flame-wing straightened and soared to a quick stop. His feet met grass.

I jumped off the animal and scurried toward the little hut on the seashore. Eaves peeked from under the hatched roof, and salt air burst through the door as I crashed into the room.

"Papa?" I pulled to a stop.

A green rug lay under a table circled by four chairs with tall backs that faced me. A ladder reached to the loft where a bedroom lay, waiting for Teion and me. I scurried up, but that room also was empty.

Splashing my face with cold water from the basin, I threw myself outside. Warm sun touched my cheeks, and the breeze made me turn to face the great Sea. Pebbles swept down to the ocean and tickled my feet as I tore off my shoes and rushed to meet the water. It splashed around my legs, and I scooped up handfuls and threw them into the air. Drops fell like rain, making me laugh. My legs collapsed, and water swept above my head. It rushed into my nose. I jerked up, snorting and laughing with dripping hair and a lopsided smile.

Then I turned, and my eyes swept across the beach. Nearby, Teion struggled to the cabin with supplies from the flame-wings, but far off down the beach, a figure stood against the wind.

"Papa!" I raced down the pebbly shore. Ground disappeared between us, and I threw myself against him. He reached down and ruffled my hair. His hands pulled me close. Warmth hugged my body.

"It was great, Papa!" I pulled away and spread my arms wide. "I got to fight on a flame-wing. We were flying like so high, and then we would dive down, and everything exploded! All the big warriors said I did really good and should go back. I'll fly forever! And Teion's gonna be an awesome prince, the best one ever!"

"Oh," he said, his face deepening with frown wrinkles. Papa pushed back dark hair lined with silver-grey and straightened to face the Sea. The sun made his skin glow like the color of red-brown clay, hidden under the stubble of a scratchy beard on his chin. His eyes never left the ocean.

I let my smaller fingers slip into his hard ones. "Are you thinking of a story, Papa?" My legs grew tight in excitement. His stories were always the best.

He nodded. "Everything is so different now."

"Tell me."

Papa knelt for a pebble on the shore, rubbing it between his thumb and forefinger. Then he drew his arm back and threw the pebble into the Sea. The rock skipped on the water, once, twice, three times. Drops flew. Fell.

"When Érkeos began, the land was perfect," he said, looking at the Sea. "Our ancestors lived in the Oasis—only a man and a woman whom the King had created and placed there. Where the four riverheads met, the trees were lush with fruit and berries clinging to every bough. You could walk and find the juiciest things to eat. And they were so soft. It was as if the entire land of Érkeos itself was made just for them."

"Mm." I squeezed my eyes shut and tried to imagine it. "Were there animals too?"

"Everywhere," he said. "Every type of animal you could imagine. Their fur was so thick. Music always filled the air, but it was the music of the birds, the trees, the animals. And when night came, the stars themselves sang a song too beautiful to describe." Papa let out his breath. "But back to the animals—they were all friendly. Our ancestors would sit under the trees in the Oasis with little creatures scrambling onto their laps. My grandfather told me a tale of when a flame-wing sat by the woman's side and fell asleep as she scratched him under his neck!"

I joined in his laughter and made a mental note to try it on my own flame-wing. But Papa's voice grew softer.

"The man and woman were so happy. They spent their lives feasting and rejoicing in life. Every day was a celebration."

"Papa," I asked, "where were you and me and Teion and everyone else? Did we live in the Oasis with them? Did we have fun with them too?"

He looked at the sky, the lines around his lips smiling. "No, my son. This was a time long ago, before our great grandfathers were born. It's history but so much more. It's *our* history. Because these were our people."

I nodded.

"The couple lived there joyfully. They explored the rivers, climbed the trees, and named all the animals. Each one was precious and loved by them."

"What about me? Did they love me too way back then?" I interrupted.

He shook his head with a slight smile. "They didn't know about you and your brothers or even me. We weren't born, silly child."

I gasped. "Where was I when I wasn't born?"

"I'm telling a story, Rekém. Will you listen?"

I gave a quick nod.

"The people loved the Oasis. It was their beautiful home, lovelier than any place you'll discover in this kingdom. But do you know what the best part was?" His throat clenched as he turned to me.

"Climbing the trees?" My eyes lit up.

"No, even better than climbing the trees." His voice softened to a whisper. "The best part was that the King walked and talked with them."

I opened my mouth to respond, but another voice severed my thoughts.

"Rekém, come on. It's time for you to go back to the cabin." Teion's face hardened as he pulled me away from Papa.

I turned halfway back to see Papa standing on the beach. Around his lips, stiff lines sunk like waves in the ocean. I cupped my hands around my mouth. "You can tell me the rest of the story later, Papa!"

Teion pushed me into the cabin and turned back to the beach. "I'm going to talk to our father. Get ready for bed now. We'll have a long day tomorrow."

"Okay, but when you get in bed, I want to tell you about flying in the battle yesterday. It was so awesome!"

He left with a grunt. I hurried to the pantry to stuff a chunk of bread in my mouth. Slipping to my loft bedroom, I brushed my hair just like Papa had shown me. I looked in our tiny mirror and stuck out my tongue. A smudge of black was dabbed on my forehead from the smoke of the day before, and I dropped the mirror onto my bed. I dug into my pocket. Grabbing a tiny piece of charcoal I saved from the battle—I found lots of cool things—I began drawing lines on my face. Black lines smudged like wrinkles, and I added a mustache on my lip. Gazing in the mirror, I grimaced and made faces until my belly hurt from laughing so hard.

I began to make shapes on my chin.

"Rekém!" Teion threw aside the charcoal and shoved me onto the bed. I somersaulted backwards with a peal of laughter until I met his dark eyes. "Clean up. I said you were supposed to be ready for bed."

My smile faded. As Teion left, I washed my face, changed into other clothes, and put the piece of charcoal back into my pocket for tomorrow. Shivering, I let the blankets crawl around me. Goosebumps dotted my legs, and I rubbed them, trying not to laugh at how ticklish they were.

The ladder creaked. I squeezed my eyes shut. Something trudged on the floorboards by my bed before the ladder creaked again. I opened my eyes, and the room was empty. Someone had thrown my dirty clothes in the corner.

A voice whispered below. I sat up. It felt like my ears pointed straight forward, but the words were too quiet to hear. Finally, a chair pushed away from the table with a high squeak, and the words grew easier to hear.

"You can't win this battle." That was Papa's voice, but it sounded like his throat was choked. Maybe he was angry.

Teion spoke even louder. "We will win. I'm the Prince; I have power bigger than you know."

There was a slight shuffling. "This is a battle you'll never win," he said again. "You don't know the King like I do."

"And you don't know your Prince like I do. Good always wins."

Papa hesitated. "Is liberation, separation from the King, good?"

Silence fell. I heard Papa sigh, and my fists clenched. I wanted to rush down there and beat Teion up for making Papa upset. But if I did, Teion would sit on me. He did it before.

"I beg you," Papa's voice cracked. I gasped when I heard something like sobs in his voice. "Don't do this, my son. But if you must, let me at least keep Rekém. He's too young."

"He's a warrior. This is what we do."

Warmth rushed over my face, and I bit my knuckles to keep from exploding. Under the blankets, I kicked my legs against the bed. I was a warrior. Teion was a Prince, and he said so!

When the voices grew softer, I slipped back onto my pillow. Darkness crept across the ceiling, and I couldn't see its pattern anymore. But Teion's voice echoed through my ears. *A warrior.*

My eyelids grew heavy, and I didn't see when Teion crawled into the other side of the bed. The night settled in cold mist. I shivered and opened my eyes. Night still covered the air, and the silent world called for me. I tiptoed down the ladder to grab another piece of bread for my empty stomach.

But before I found my snack, a faint light came through the still-open door. I slipped into the salty Sea air. A thousand stars shone and shot across the sky, every reflection sparkling on the waves.

A hand touched me, pulled me close. I let the hair on Papa's beard brush my cheek as he knelt beside me.

"Rekém." His voice was soft like the mist. "I never got to finish my story."

I yawned and turned toward him. "You can tell me tomorrow. I just want to eat and go back to bed now." My legs stumbled to the pantry.

He waited as I grabbed my bread, but his fingers reached for mine. "This story is important. I must tell you now."

6

and He embraces lost prayers

A sweet smell danced through the blackness like the stray honeysuckles I found once on an old wall. But when I sniffed the honeysuckles, the wall scratched my skin, and now I felt something else cutting my cheek. Somehow, I couldn't push away. Colors flashed into vision. Pretty purple mixed with black. Tiny lights glowed beyond it, like the stars, but I couldn't reach them. When my eyes turned toward the sparkles, they danced away. I grasped for them but slipped.

A noise touched my ears. Children begged to see something; their feet crunched on gravel. A voice like my own mama's hushed their words, and I tried to see what they saw. Hear what they heard.

Something touched me. The warmth brushed my shoulder and lifted me off the ground. Air kissed my stinging face, the sun shining on my closed lids. Arms pulled me tight.

"Ka-Daddy?" My cracked lips whispered. I snuggled closer into the strong chest. My ear pressed against his shirt, and the sound of his heart filled mine.

Ka-Daddy was carrying me like he always did. We would tiptoe into the desert night to where the torch guarded our city. In silence, Ka-Daddy would take down the wick as it grew low and hand it to Ka-Mama. All three of us—the Torch Keepers for the King. Once more, blue fire would cut away the enemy and defend our gates. And Ka-Daddy would bring me in his arms and lay me down to sleep.

But these arms weren't his. They were stronger somehow. And the shirt smelled like wood dust mixed with flowers.

A voice spoke. "Peace, child." The arms held me tight, and a hand brushed my cheek. Light dimmed to a warm twinkle. It was like the sun but a different color—a soft blue surrounding me like the sky. Maybe I was flying.

The arms slipped me into silky blankets—or were they clouds? Quilts pulled tight yet gentle around my shoulders. Something cool and damp touched my forehead. I jerked.

"Peace, my child."

Curled in the blankets, I let the blackness cover me again. But, as the colors faded, the distant stars came nearer again. They began to glow brighter and brighter. My eyes burned. And then I saw her.

Ka-Mama.

She disappeared, and I began to cry.

The sound of humming pulled me out of my dreams. I lay against a thick pillow and listened to the gentle song, like Ka-Mama always sang. But when I opened my eyes, I jerked blankets tight around my shoulders.

The room glowed. On a candle stand, a flame burned blue and cast pale light on the white walls. The candle made everything turn funny colors, like the little pictures dotting the wall and the carpet on the ground that looked scratchy. My eyebrows pulled tight. I let my feet slip into the carpet's fingers and crept toward the first picture.

A child's hand had drawn a butterfly's golden wings as it flew on the thing Ka-Mama had called a tree. The picture next to it just looked like scribble scrabble. And then the third one. It showed the top of a house smiling with pink flowers. Two people stood near the door, their faces arched happy like a rainbow.

I touched the taller figure. The lady's hand reached down to a child beside her, and I swallowed a lump in my throat.

"Ka-Mama."

A hug reached around my shoulders. Breath touched my ear.

"Good morning, dear."

I twisted away and glared in the strange face. Silvery-white hair lined thin cheeks that were etched with wrinkles. A brown spot on her cheek like a freckle quivered when she smiled at me.

"I want Ka-Mama." I pulled away from the old stranger and ran to the bed. But as I reached up, I found it was too tall for me to climb back into. I hid my face in the blanket.

Her footsteps drew near, but she didn't hug me this time. "Your mother is not here, my dear, but we will do everything we can to find her. Are you hungry? Come and sit with me."

I let her take my hand and lead me out of the blue bedroom. A table was spread in the next room near a fireplace. Windows opened wide to let in fresh air, and a propped-open door showed me an arch with pretty flowers. Beyond that, my eyes caught the alley where Ka-Mama had disappeared.

"Come, dear." The woman sat in a rocking chair and motioned for me to take a smaller seat beside her.

I froze. My eyes turned toward the door and beyond. My heart felt like someone twisted it hard. As a slice of wind cut against the flowers, I flung myself out the door.

The woman called behind me, but my feet ran past the rocky ground. Light raced away from me as I left the house behind. The ground became wet and stinky. I ran to the end of the alley and turned right. Or maybe it was left; I wasn't sure. My fists clenched as I tried to remember where Ka-Mama had brought me. At another street, I stopped. To my left, the city wall stood tall against green plants that peeked at me, high and twisted with pointy things like needles on the top. They looked like cactus plants except the thorns were softer and fuzzy—were they different types of trees? I raced to the wall anyway and touched the grey stones. My fingers traced their rough ends as I ran away from the morning sun.

And there—a break! I fell to my knees, and they scraped against the sharp rocks. With all my strength, I tried to shove the wall forward like my mama had. But it stood strong.

"Ka-Mama!" My breaths came in gasps. I let my hands fall, and I collapsed against the wall. The sun burned my back as I shook, crying. I felt my mama's necklace still around my neck, and the tears fell faster.

"My child?" A deep voice called out to me. It was the one from the dream, a voice like Ka-Daddy's. I turned toward it and let myself run into a man's thick arms. He dropped a walking stick to the ground, pulling me tight. The man rocked back and forth on his heels.

Tears fell hot down my cheeks. "I want my mama and daddy."

He didn't answer, only continued to rock. I took a deep breath and pointed back at the wall. "Ka-Mama went there. I wanna find her."

His eyes met mine. Under a soft beard of red-brown, he smiled.

"Peace, my child."

I relaxed in his arms. The man bent to pick up his stick again. Gently, he carried me away from the wall and back toward the flower house. With every crunch of his feet, there was also a rhythmic touch of a stick against gravel. I tried to keep back the tears, but they fell anyway. As I buried my eyes away from the world, we turned to the arch of flowers, and the older lady rushed toward us.

"My son, you found her? Oh, I was so worried—,"

Other children peeked from behind the flowers and stared at me. I looked at them and then hid my face in the man's chest again, ignoring their whisperings. With my eyes pressed shut, I only thought of Ka-Mama and how she would hold me tight when I was scared. Why wasn't she here this time?

"And then I found this," the woman said. I twisted around to see her pull out a dark bottle.

I tried to grab it. "That's mine! Ka-Daddy gave it to me."

She hesitated. "What did he do with it?"

My lips pressed tight. I turned to stare into the eyes of the man. I jerked in surprise. His eyes were blue. Just like my own daddy's. Like mine.

He nodded.

"Ka-Mama put the drops in my eyes," I said, "so the enemy wouldn't know."

"Know what?"

My chin fell, and I choked out the words. "That my eyes are blue like Ka-Daddy's."

The older woman drew in her breath quickly. "Then it's true. The secret door in the wall, the eyes... we must talk with Emyir. She would know."

"Not now." The man's deep voice made his chest quiver, and I jerked. When I turned to see his face, he whispered a breath. "Peace, child. What is your name?"

I looked into his eyes. "Ka-Dara."

He smiled. "Kadira. My little friend."

The man didn't put a pause between my names. I opened my mouth to correct him, to tell him that I was Ka-Dara, with the same first name as my mama and daddy. But his eyes were so happy when he looked at me. Instead, I closed my lips and nodded. *Kadira.*

The man took me into the house and sat me in his lap. There, sitting a few steps from the fire, we rocked in silence. Blue flames crept up and warmed a pot that filled the air with yummy smells. When a cup was filled for me, I blew on it and drank a little. The hot tea was a little spicy yet sweet on my tongue.

"Kadira, my child," the man said, "I am called Father. You may call me that as well if you choose."

I didn't say anything. Drinking more tea, I looked back at the fire. My body jerked. Every time I saw the flames, I thought of the last night I lit the torch with Ka-Mama. And then I saw Ka-Mama's face growing distant with a whisper, "Be brave."

7

Rekém

in night's darkness, eternity's pen etches numbers, dates;
every neglected century erased

Papa pulled me beside him, our shoulders touching. We sat in the doorway with our faces turned to the great Sea. Its breeze touched our cheeks, and the stars shone high above. The rest was darkness.

"Our ancestors' story," Papa began. "It started in the Oasis, remember? Our people were so happy. There was peace, and they had everything. But that wasn't enough."

My lips twisted. "Everything wasn't enough?"

He chuckled. "It'll make sense when you're older, Rekém. The couple wanted more. And so the first man became an imposter. He thought he could get what he wanted, and he chose his own way instead of following the way of the King."

"He was a bad man then!"

"Yes," he sighed, "but no. Because somehow, we're all like him. That man became the first Prince. He wanted to overthrow the kingdom, but no man can be more powerful than the King. And because our ancestors disobeyed, punishment had to follow. The King—." His voice stilled.

"What did he do? Was the King mean?" My eyes narrowed.

"No, Rekém. He was kind. But because the new Prince and his wife disobeyed, they had to leave their home. The King ignited a wall of fire around the Oasis so no one could ever go back. And I always wonder... wonder what if our people had simply obeyed."

My forehead wrinkled. "But Papa, I disobey, and you still love me."

"Yes," he said, "and the King still loves us. But I always wonder what the King thought when he looked at his people who rebelled. Did his eyes burn like fire? Or did he cry, somehow hurting for his lost children?"

I snorted. "King's don't cry. They're brave."

"I don't know."

When Papa didn't say anything for a while, I let out a big breath. "Well, I like stories, but I'm sleepy too. And if this happened a long time ago," I stopped and stared. "Wait. That man became the first Prince. Does that mean he was Teion?"

He shook his head. "No, there have been many Princes, rising and falling. Érkeos has two types of men—those who love the King's old stories and those who hate them. You can only choose for yourself, and Teion has chosen his way."

"Papa," I said, "being a prince is really cool. Why aren't you one?"

His fingers turned my chin to look straight into his face. "No honor is greater than being a servant of the King's way, my son."

I rubbed at my eyebrow and looked away.

"It comes with a price. I have sought the Oasis and the King, and I lost much. Your mother did not believe the stories, and she fled because it was too hard to be together. She stole our third son and disappeared. To start over. You too may have loss if you follow the King's ways, but it is always worth the pain."

I leaned my chin onto my fist. My forehead grew tight. The words tumbled through my head, but they couldn't seem to connect.

"Don't forget, Rekém." He leaned forward. "Don't forget the Oasis. There is so much I do not understand, but never forget the Oasis and where our people came from. And my son, when you are confused, go find our roots and remain there. Find the four riverheads that flowed into the Oasis. When you find where the moon-flower grows, you will be there."

I shrugged. "Okay, Papa. I'll find it one day, but first I want to fly on the flame-wings. It's so cool. We were super high in the air, and it was like I was flying!"

A shadow passed over his face. "It's your decision, my son."

I yawned. "Good night, Papa. I'll see you in the morning."

"Good night, Rekém." He hesitated before pressing a kiss against my hair, tight. I looked in his face as I pulled away. When did Papa kiss me before?

Entering the house, I collapsed beside Teion's sleeping body. Thoughts washed through my brain. I thought of the King and how he chased my papa's great, great, great—and more greats—grandfather and his wife off their own land. The Prince stood there watching the tower of fire push him from his home. Did he cry?

Of course he didn't. Men were stronger than that. Kings and Princes never cried. But I still stared in the darkness and wondered.

How could a good King do that? Couldn't he just forgive them for their mistakes like Papa forgave me?

I tossed and turned in the darkness until it swallowed me up.

Air swept past me as I flew on the back of a flame-wing in my dreams. Then something shook. The world tumbled around, dissolved in a sharp *hiss.*

"Wake up!" Teion appeared above me. Large circles hung under his eyes as he jerked my body with each move of his arms.

I rolled over and tried to bury myself under the blankets. Teion grabbed them away and pulled me to the cold floor. No birds sang in the still-dark morning.

"Come on. It's time to go."

I stumbled after him. A sliver on the ladder broke through the fleshy part of my foot, and I fell down the rest of the steps with a yell. My fingernails dug for the splinter. It came out with a drop of blood.

Teion jerked me to my feet. "No dawdling. The flame-wings are waiting."

"The flame-wings!" I beat him out the door as I found my mount sleeping. A rumbling grew in his throat as I slipped onto the scaly back and adjusted to the most comfortable position.

When Teion sank on his own beast, I turned to him. "Is Papa coming too?"

He laughed, and it thundered through his chest like an earthquake. Teion's flame-wing stood and shook its head. Teion straightened. "He's gone. He left us last night."

"No!" I tried to scramble off my flame-wing, but Teion grabbed me and jerked me back on. I pointed towards the cabin. "Papa didn't leave. I was talking to him. I told Papa I'd see him this morning!"

He struck me against the mouth. I fell backwards. My hand rushed to my lips and came back with sticky blood.

"Don't contradict me, boy." He snapped a rope against his flame-wing, and the animal straightened with a half-concealed growl. "It's the same with those who follow the way of the King like our father. They're all liars."

My mind flashed to the stories Papa told me. How could Papa serve a King who let those bad things happen to him? I would never do that. If I followed Teion, I could fly all the time and fight big battles!

My flame-wing burst to life. Its claws left the soil, and I found myself swirling up, climbing straight into the clouds. My hands burned, and my knees struggled to hold on. For a second, I looked back to the ground and imagined what it would feel like to fall.

A speck of green rose from where our cabin stood. I gawked to see flames of fire burst up. Deep smoke stained the air as our house caught in a blaze. The fire grew, billowed, and then disappeared as we left behind the Sea and the forests and the green, entering only the dusty dryness of the desert.

And I looked back and wondered where Papa was and why he left us.

8

KADIRA

silent tears arousing redemption's song,
but she can't hear it

I sat at a big table. My elbows scratched against wood, but the other children didn't notice me. They shoved the last pieces of bread into their mouths and raced out the door. Their laughter danced like Ka-Mama and I used to dance.

I stared at the dead fire, then down to my plate. The bread thing wasn't like what Ka-Mama made for me. This stuff was hard, crusty, and something brown and sweet was drizzled inside. But my stomach lurched.

Gamma hummed as she collected the plates. When she reached me, I hid my face.

"Kadira," she said, "would you like to go play?"

I looked hard at the plate and ignored her voice. I didn't want to play. I just wanted Ka-Mama to come back, Ka-Daddy to pick me up and call me his little princess. I wanted to feel my mama's tummy and talk to our baby and run in the sand with my real friends. Not these dark eyes that always watched me.

"You can go outside if you'd like, my dear. Just stay close, please." Gamma slipped my plate away.

I nodded, but my chin held close to my chest. Rising, I walked slowly to the door. The sunlight cut my face. I looked down the street to where I could run away and find Ka-Daddy and Ka-Mama. But they'd come back for me soon. Until then, I'd be a Torch Keeper here, with the lady called Emyir, so Ka-Mama would be proud of me.

The children's voices called from behind the house. I stumbled away, toward my left where a wooden building lay by the city wall. Away from those laughing faces, I hid by the shop. Kneeling, I peered through two boards.

Inside, three flickering candles chased shadows into corners and under the benches that were pushed to the side of the room. Half-hewn chairs lay beside knives and other sharp things as if waiting for someone's hands to turn them into what they were intended to be. I studied the strange bits of wood and dust that covered each workbench—works in progress.

A staff swung before my eyes. I covered my mouth to keep from screaming. The roof arched above the man who was called Father, and he held a stick in both hands, hesitating before thrusting it forward in a sharp arc. With a flick of his wrist, the staff danced on his palm and twirled in the air. It swung around and around so quickly that my eyes couldn't see where his hands had gone. And then in a moment, all stilled as he pulled it up sharp. His body grew silent. The man turned toward me. His blue eyes saw me right through the wall, I knew somehow.

I pulled away and ran to hide. Behind the home and the shop, there was a backyard where children ran toward a tall tree in the corner. I sank against the house and turned my eyes toward them. But the shop's door opened. The man walked out, his chest heaving in and out as he flexed the bow staff. When Father saw me, he smiled. I watched until he disappeared behind the corner. My shoulders trembled.

A boy yelled as he scrambled into the tall tree. I pulled my body tight against the wall, watching him. He leaned out on a branch with one hand free, his black shoes pressed against the tree trunk. When he called to a group of girls below, they clapped at how brave he was. Then he turned to stare at me, and the others did too. Everyone did that.

I looked back at the ground. Grass scratched my leg, and I brushed it away. A bug began to crawl up my foot, and I gasped as I shook it off.

"Kadira?" A quiet voice asked by my side.

I jerked my head up to look up at a boy my size who wore a large smile. His grin grew until I could see every tooth and the dark places where some were missing, and his cheeks bulged.

"We're gonna go on a walk. Father and Gamma told me to get everyone. I'll show you my favorite spots!"

I shook my head.

"Come 'n! It'll be fun." He grinned and held out a hand.

I looked at him and swallowed hard. His smile reminded me of Am-Othniel, and, for some reason, that made my neck hurt with a weird ache.

I nodded and let him pull me up. The boy quickly called the other children, and four of them scrambled to the street where the adults waited. But the boy with funny teeth waited by my side.

He grinned. "You have pretty eyes. They're really dark brown, like dirt." His face turned red. "But I mean that's a good thing! Dirt is really nice."

I smiled a little, but then turned away. Something hurt inside my tummy. My eyes *weren't* brown. Ka-Mama told me to hide their real color with the moon-flower juice. To hide the blueness. No one would ever know my secrets.

"This is awkward," the boy said, rubbing the edge of his mouth, "so I'll tell you my name. I'm Ike." He gave a little bow.

I stared at him. "What's your first name?"

He laughed. He did that a lot, it seemed. "I don't have one."

"Everyone has one."

"Not me." Ike tilted his head to the side. "My parents both died. Father and Gamma adopted me into their family, and they don't have a first name."

I stared. "Why not?"

"'Cause." He shrugged. "They don't need one. None of us do. We can all be a part of the same big family with a dad and a grandma!"

I shook my head. We walked together without saying anything. Ike's words were so confusing. He waited for me to say something, but, when I didn't, he kept talking. "I like you. You're a good sister. And I think we'll have fun playing."

"I'm not your sister," I said.

Ike laughed. "We can pretend then. We're all family now—you, me, Father, Gamma, and everyone else."

I raised my eyes to his face. His pale cheeks grinned at me as we followed the rest of the group.

"Ka-Mama's coming back," I said, loud. "She'll bring me home, so I can't stay here."

Ike's smile didn't fade. "Then we can have fun 'til she brings you home!"

"Come 'n, Ike! Let's race!" the boy with black shoes called out, and Ike beamed at me.

"I'll show you my favorite spots when we get there." He turned to the other boy and let go of my hand. "Coming, Faine!"

I crossed my arms, my hand suddenly feeling cold. Letting my hair fall over my eyes, I watched the group before me. The silver-haired woman kept an eye out on all of us, and three girls tried to cling to her at the same time. We were supposed to call her Gamma, she said. But I bit my lip and trudged forward.

By my side, I sensed the taller man—Father—meet me. His staff plodded as he walked slowly without speaking, taking my hand in his. I looked up at his blue eyes and curly, brown beard, and he smiled.

He wasn't Ka-Daddy. But I could call him Father, and that was okay.

Turning a corner, the street ended and turned into a big open place. People walked everywhere. Noises filled my ears, but I ignored them. On one end of the town square, I saw a great dancehall with tall, glass windows. The door cracked open, and I gasped.

"Oth!" I lunged forward.

Gamma was by my side in an instant. "What's wrong, dear?"

"My friend Am-Othniel is in there." I pointed at the dancehall and tried to pull away. "He plays the instruments. I wanna see him."

"He's not here. Your friend is in your city, remember?" Her voice lowered gently, and the freckle in her cheek deepened, "But we will try to find him, dear."

We walked away from the square, but my eyes stared behind us. I watched the towering dancehall until it was hidden, lost in the city. And then my shoulders sank.

My friends were gone. Am-Othniel and Ir-Ivah and Ir-Haran. Everything was gone. My throat hurt again.

Father squeezed my hand. I turned back and tried to forget the memories. But they kept coming.

"Ka-Mama," I whispered so Father couldn't hear me, "I'm scared."

Suddenly, the city gates opened wide before us. I gasped. It was just like home. My legs raced forward. Twisting around people, I hurried toward the torch. My neck stretched up to see it as the fire burned straight and tall before the city walls. Blue fire mixed with gold sunshine. And I stared at the city gates where curved writing was etched in the stone. Slowly, I sounded out the letters.

"Pa-la-tiel." I stopped. "Oh." My shoulders lowered. It wasn't my home.

"The mountain pass." Another voice joined mine.

I turned to see the whole group near me, but a new person had joined them. A small woman with dusty hair and blue eyes knelt by my side. She touched me.

"I am Emyir, keeper of the fire. I hear you are a Torch Keeper as well."

"No, Ka-Mama and Ka-Daddy are," I said. "But I will be when I grow up."

She smiled. "One is never too young to embrace their calling. And I'd be pleased if you joined me one day."

I chewed on my cheek and grew silent. Emyir stood and motioned to Gamma and Father. They stepped aside, but I listened to their quiet voices. The words cut the brave feelings I tried to hold onto.

"Her parents... the Liberation... everything burned. They're all killed—murdered."

I sank to the mountain stones as the last words cut through me.

"The only one who escaped."

Ike grabbed my hand and offered a smile, but I pushed him off. Staring up at the torch, my head shook back and forth. It wasn't true. They were all lies. Ka-Mama said she'd come back for me. She promised.

Then why was I crying?

9

KADIRA

*where will she be brought out
when so far away?*

It was so dark. Shadows crawled on the wall and on the shapes of colored pictures that were now only black. Except that white piece. It flickered in the breath of air. And a spark—there under the mirror—a tiny flash of light. Was it my bottle of moon-flower juice? I grabbed the blankets around my chin. Something creaked outside the door.

"Ka-Mama?" I called. When there was no answer, I sat all the way up. Maybe I missed her answer. "Ka-Mama?" I said again.

The floorboards groaned again, but she wasn't there. I pushed myself back so my shoulders rested against my pillows. Pulling the blankets around my knees, I waited.

A new sound came. At first, I heard the tremble of soft wind. The roof shook as the wind hit harder. I shivered, but sandstorms came a lot in the desert. Ka-Daddy told me that the King would keep me safe.

I paused and nibbled on the corner of the blanket. Looking into the darkness, my forehead pulled tight.

Why didn't the King keep Ka-Daddy and Ka-Mama safe? Did he lie?

Something rumbled, like when my tummy made funny noises, but this was deeper. It began low and then got louder.

And then a crash. Light lit up the room, pale and yellow.

I screamed and dove under the blankets. More flashes exploded around the house. All Érkeos seemed to twist and shake.

I covered my eyes and rolled into a tight ball. Along with the crashing noise came a loud pounding on the roof.

I jumped off the bed and tried to shove myself under it. Wiggling into the darkness, my breathing came in gasps.

They were back—the people who chased me and Ka-Mama. They would explode our world. They would kill us!

My body shook as I cried and hid under the bed. And then someone reached for me.

"Go away!" I tried to shake the blanket at them. "Give me back my mama! I want her! You meanie, I hate you, I hate you!" My words stopped as tears fell.

"My child. My Kadira," Father said. He knelt and pulled me from the darkness. Gently lifting me against his chest, I threw myself into his arms and sobbed. He took me from the bedroom to the place where the fire burned with a white-blue light.

I tried to pull away, but he held me there. I felt his lips against my hair like Ka-Daddy always kissed me when I was scared. Father walked back and forth before the fire, whispering in my hair.

"You are safe, my child. Be still." His arms crept around my back, strong.

But the crashing came again. The room lit up in blinding light, and my body shook with quivers. I wanted to lunge back under the bed, to hide, to escape.

"They-They're gonna get us." I whimpered between sobs. "Like they got me and Ka-Mama. They'll burn everything and kill us."

I looked in his face. Strangely, a smile crept under his brown beard. He knelt and let me stand before him, shivering. Wrapping my blanket around me, he put both hands on my shoulders.

"My child," he said, "You are safe. Nothing can touch you when I am here. You must trust."

My jaw quivered. "But they took away my daddy and mama."

He nodded, and a shadow came across his forehead. "Your King has a plan. He has a purpose."

"I don't think—." I hesitated, chewing on the back of my knuckles. "I don't think I like his plan very much." I looked up quickly. "Is that super bad?"

Lines creased his face. "The King still loves you." He stood. "Let me show you, my child."

He still held me in his arms as he walked toward the door. Opening it slowly, the outside world met us in a breath of cold air. The flashing light had gone, but the loud pounding continued. In the light of the fire, I saw the enemy—only drops of water falling onto the roof.

The rumbling sounded, but it was far away. Father smiled. "This is a rain storm, and you are safe."

79

I gasped. "Water is falling from the sky." Looking at Father's smiling face, I let out my breath. "It doesn't do this at home."

He chuckled and pressed his cheek against mine. "Do you like it?"

"I...I think I like it." My eyes turned toward his. "Can I...?"

He nodded.

I wiggled out of Father's arms, and our hands met. Taking the first step, my feet met wet ground. Drops slid down my nose. I laughed as Father pulled me out into the rain, and we danced. In the starless night our feet splashed in puddles, Father twirled me under his arm, and then he slipped, falling onto the grass. We laughed so hard that my sides hurt. I jumped to sit beside him. His arm crept around me, and we sat under the rain and got wet and didn't care because somehow it was perfect and beautiful.

I patted his beard. "You're super wet!"

He shook his head like a wet animal, and water went everywhere. I blinked and giggled. "I like this rain," I said. "It's fun."

He rubbed water off my forehead. "The King made it for you. He knew you'd dance in it. He knew you'd love it."

My mouth gaped. "Really? How'd he know?"

"He just does," Father said. "He loves you."

I grew serious. "Does the King know I was scared of his rain?"

"Yes." He nodded soberly. "But that's okay. A lot of people's fears are silly when they realize it. But the King knows, and he loves anyway."

"Big people too?"

"Especially big people."

I stood and looked down at him without smiling. For several seconds, our eyes met. His blue ones were like Ka-Daddy's. I swallowed. "Father?"

He pressed my hand.

"I—." That burning feeling came in my neck. I swallowed, and tears mixed with rain. "I miss my daddy."

He rose and pressed me close. "I know. The King gave you a daddy for an important reason." Our gazes joined. "But now he's gone." Father let my feet touch the ground, and he knelt, taking my palm in his. Water trailed down his cheeks into his beard as he kissed the back of my hand. "My child, will you let me take his place?"

I inhaled quickly.

"And until the day when the King brings you and your daddy together again, can I hold you when you cry? Can I dance with you and know your secrets and share my home with you? My child," he said, "I love you."

I cried and let him hug me again. Father took me inside where we curled cross-legged before the fire and drank something warm that made steam in the air. And there, hiding on his lap with his fingers caressing my hair, I nodded.

Under my breath, I whispered, "I miss you, Ka-Mama." I stopped and shook my head. "I miss you, *Mama* and *Daddy*." My body relaxed. Somehow, leaving out our first name was nicer. Maybe we could all be part of Father and Gamma's family.

CRR

10

Rekém

searching for more,
finding less

One year later...

If one could slice the air, my flame-wing and I were like a knife cutting through its fingers. A hundred wings flew behind me in perfect syncopation. My knees held tight around my own creature's leathery hide, and I pulled an arrow from a quiver. It was only a practice arrow, a narrow shaft with pointed eyes at the razor head that waited to cut the air in two. Sadly, this arrow wouldn't explode on contact like the ones we used in real battles. But I locked it in my bow. Ready. Watching.

At the head of the aviation fleet, I threw my arms back. My black hair had grown long over the last year to hang nipping at my shoulders, but the wind shoved my bangs away from my eyes. I tensed.

And then the flame-wing dropped. We fell with the speed of gravity. Distance disappeared, and the land rushed to meet us. All I could feel was cold air against my cheeks. Earth growing. Heart pounding.

A war cry left my throat, and I pulled the flame-wing up. We leveled up to soar just above the dusty ground. Every pulse of the creature's body mirrored the pounding in my heart, and the leathery wings almost scraped the sandy desert. The ground shot behind us as we headed like an arrow straight between two scraggly cacti. They rushed forward, tall and green, spines staring at us like knives ready to impale our lungs. I inhaled sharply.

In an instant, the flame-wing twisted vertically. I released two arrows. They flew. Cut. Pierced.

We slowed as I turned half-way around. My arrows joined the volley of spines embedded in the cacti. The fletching shook for a moment as we shot by, then grew still. And behind me, my trainees copied my movement. A handful of stray arrows flew harmlessly in the air, but our targets grew heavy with quivering feathers.

And we climbed again. We met the clouds and disappeared in white fog that swirled around us. It curled, glided in gentle mist. As the last rider left Érkeos, we hesitated in the cool vapor before descending into hot air once again. Dampness clung to my hair, and the breath of the clouds clung to my upper lip like a mustache. I looked back to the earth and marked the path we had soared. How many scores of furlongs had we traveled in seconds?

When the flame-wings landed in the sand, a cloud of dust rose around us. My comrades clapped their arms around each other and compared the number of arrows each had shot. I slipped away from my students and found the solitary figure who stood against the desert.

"Pretty good practice, huh?" I joined Teion's side and surveyed my group. Fifty men dressed in grey-black tunics, their hair messed by the wind, threw down their bows and began to tend to their mounts. Far behind us lay the cacti, one knocked down and lying in the sand. If only the arrow shafts had been filled with exploding powder, what a sound that would have made!

Teion grunted. He grabbed the bow on my shoulder and shoved it backward. I stumbled, grabbed him for balance. My eyes met his black ones.

"We're not playing, Rekém," he hissed between his teeth.

My chin met my chest. I rubbed the sweat off my upper lip. "I know," I said through clenched teeth. "How many battles have I fought these last years? How many captives have I destroyed with my flame-wing? How many escapees have I stopped?"

"And yet you still act as if it's a big joke."

"What?" I gasped.

His voice rose. "Rekém, you're either all in or all out. Sure, you can do tricks on your flying butterfly, but when are you going to grow up?" He shoved something against my chest. "When will you fight like a man?"

I looked down at the knife in his fist. My hands recoiled, but they slowly rose to touch the hot metal. I slipped it into my belt.

Teion turned half-way around but stopped. When he looked back at me, fire glittered in his eyes.

"I have a mission for you, little brother."

My mouth dropped open. "Me? What is it? I'll go right away!"

He snorted and shook his head. "Grow up. It's not adventures and games, Rekém."

I stiffened.

"It's been said that some of the blue-eyed ones have escaped from the cities we've raided. They are loyal to the King and enemies to our Liberation. They must be brought down." He clapped my shoulder with a hard hand. "Those with blue eyes are specially selected by the King, and they encourage their towns to follow his narrow ways. If they are destroyed, the cities also will fall." He stepped away and raised his voice. "You'll be sent to the edge of the mountains to search out the villages there. See if the rumors are true. And if they are," he motioned to the knife, "kill any who will not turn."

"To the mountains," I said. When I caught Teion's glare, I jerked my chin up and gave a sharp nod. "Yes, my prince. I'll leave immediately."

I turned to my flame-wing, but Teion stopped me with a mocking laugh.

"You won't be needing that beast. This time you don't get an army. You're not a general like I am, so mount a sabbax like the rest of the amateur fighters. Just see if you can prove yourself, little brother." His jaw tightened.

"I will." My eyes hesitated on my flame-wing. The animal's jaw lowered as he waited for me to mount and escape into the skies again. Wings folded. Paused.

I felt my chest quiver. Turning away, I ran past Teion. My army of riders was already gone, and I left my beast to sit in the sand waiting for me. And I wouldn't come back.

My flame-wing called, the smooth, gentle noise rocking through me like the purring of a cat, but I ignored him. I ran across the sand and into the encampment's corrals.

Sabbax deer chewed on dried grasses and raised their heads to look at me. Their spindly legs quivered like they would snap if I let my full weight rest on their backs. The deer's pale, thin faces were pinched with hunger, and their bones poked out like sticks. I slapped one on its rear, and he jerked away, tripping over another one of those miserable creatures.

I sensed Teion's gaze on me. The animal handler slipped a rope into my grasp, and I mounted the already-packed animal. With a nudge of my heels, the sabbax trotted down the dunes and into the bleak, desert horizon.

I looked back, but no one waited to wave me off on my first solo mission. I reached up and felt the quiver of arrows still wrapped around my shoulder. I shoved it off to fall onto the sand, and we rode. When I looked back, the quiver already was hidden beneath the billows of sand. Only the knife hilt pressed against my stomach as we lurched forward.

I raised my eyes to the clouds and imagined the sky's dew drops against my face. Dry dust clung to my hair, but high above the desert, where I belonged, the air was cool and moist. Like the Sea I lived by as a child.

But now I was a man. A warrior like Teion said I was.

At each village and town I encountered, I paused to slip through and scan the eyes of those within. Deep browns and blacks met my own. Everyone lived his own life. No one spoke to me as I refilled my water flask and continued my way. It was as if we lived in our own worlds, and a wall rose up to separate us from another creature who might become a friend.

So I rode on. Only me and the sabbax. In the lonely world, the sun burned my skin, but I pressed forward to make my brother proud of me. And to destroy the King who had deserted my parents.

11

a noiseless yearning,
one's never-ending escape

I slipped on the new dress Gamma had made for me and then spun before a mirror. The dress's dark, nut-brown color matched my eyes, and the hem swung close around my ankles, almost tickling. Each smooth crease shivered as I twirled then suddenly stood still. My reflection stared back at me. I pulled my curly hair away from my face and tied it back with a red ribbon. But I couldn't hide from the mirror. I was eight years old, nearly grown up now. The mirror told me so. My chin was sharp, cheekbones high, and eyes dull. I fastened on my mama's necklace, and it hung cold on my throat. It was like the last party I had prepared to attend. The celebration that never happened. But this time Mama wasn't here.

The King had created our land and set apart the first two people as Torch Keepers on this day long ago. We were supposed to celebrate, but how could I when the King let Mama and Daddy die? One year had passed. Could I just move on and celebrate the day when the desert had exploded in death? When I lost Mama and Daddy?

My lips pulled tight, and I turned away. Tilting my jaw, I let a drop of the moon-flower juice stain my eyes. The sting didn't come this time. I blinked, watching my image in the mirror. My eyes darkened to near black.

I leaned toward the candle and blew it out. Light ran away. I tiptoed through the room, reaching my hands out in the darkness. When I opened the door, still blue light shone in the air from the fireplace. Already, the other children were gone.

My eyes trailed over ribbons and flowers that littered the table. A slipper hid under a chair. I looked past it. The door shook, opened slightly in the darkening purple night.

And I slipped out under the stars. The flowers over the walkway were now shadows blotting the sky. Looking between them, I tried to find the skies.

Stars seemed to shine in the darkness like glitter on a table. It was a celebration day after all. But still, the sky felt empty. No moon was there to light the night. I traced the paths of the stars, remembering the constellations Mama drew out for me in the sky so long ago. The one right above me was a Flame-wing, some sort of weird dragon animal. Mama said they were real, but they probably weren't. I knew, because she also said she loved me, then left anyway. Both were lies.

I looked away. It was another anniversary of the nation's birth. Another year gone. And yet nothing changed. Mama and Daddy were still gone, and I was still alone. I swallowed hard.

But then I heard a voice. From the carpentry shop, the door opened, and Father stepped out. He walked toward me, a light shining in the way his lips turned up under his beard.

Father squeezed my shoulder, and I tried to smile.

"You're beautiful, my child. A princess."

I looked up at him and then away. "Thanks, Father."

He paused and waited. I kicked the rocks by my feet.

"I—I don't really feel like dancing tonight." I rocked my head from side to side. "I mean, I just want to... to be alone." I blushed. "Is that okay?"

His gaze sank into me as if he saw me from the inside out. Speaking quietly, he let go of my shoulder. "Of course, my child"

I leaned against him. Father kissed the top of my hair, and I inhaled his sweet, woody smell. But I blinked hard. He could never really be Daddy. When his arms released me, I slipped away, wrapping my arms tight around my chest.

I entered the streets, and music floated on the air. Following the lights, I came to the center of the city, where voices were raised in singing and feet danced to the rhythm of the songs. But that wasn't the same either—Am-Othniel should have been the one making music.

Cold air brushed my face, and I shivered.

At the edge of the square, the world erupted in bright lights. Blues and whites shone from a circle of torches that covered the street in color. Beyond, the dancehall overflowed with swishing skirts and laughing voices.

"Kadira!" A voice called. I turned as Ike ran out of the hall, a smile on his face. "I was waiting for you. Will you dance?"

A million memories burned my mind. I ground my teeth together and ignored the weird, twisting feeling growing in my stomach. Looking away, I shook my head. "I don't dance."

"That's okay; I'll teach you."

I glanced back at the sky. There were no explosions, no burning fire that stole my hopes and future. But the coldness still clung to my bare arms. I turned away without speaking.

"Kadira!" Ike called, but I left him behind. Hurrying down a street, I moved away from the music and lights. My dress brushed my legs. I pulled it up and ran through the empty roads.

At the city gate, my thoughts grew still. The darkness stretched on forever. No armies or danger, no rushing into the desert holding to my mama's waist.

The same blue flame shone at the gate of the city. The torch fought the evil that clung to my thoughts, the memories that burned. But it couldn't erase them.

Emyir appeared by my side. "It is time."

The Torch Keeper and I walked toward the flame. My hands stilled as I took the torch off its stand and knelt on the rocky ground. Emyir touched the new wick to the old, and the torch burst into life.

She lifted the new torch high in the air. It cast light on the mountain road before us and the trees growing on the hillside. But inside, I felt as empty as the desert that was too far away to see.

"Don't you love it?" she asked.

I jerked. "What?"

Emyir knelt beside me and pressed her cheek to mine so our eyes looked together. The blue fire rose before us.

"That the King has blessed us with a task most honored in the kingdom. This torch stands because you set it here. Because you kept it lit, just like the first Torch Keepers of long ago."

I shook my head. "I only helped."

"No," Emyir smiled, "you did more than help. The King has called you, as he has called others. Some turn away in rebellion to the Prince's side, but a select few, like you, are faithful. Kadira," she hugged me, "the King loves you so much."

I looked away. If the King really knew who I was, would he still love me?

"Now," Emyir said, "go join the dance, Kadira."

I shrugged.

Emyir touched my chin and turned it to hers. Her pale eyes sparkled, and I smelled faint lavender. "Life is too precious to live in the past."

"It's not that," I began.

"No, it's that you haven't realized something," she said. "The King gave us this celebration to enjoy, to be rejuvenated. Without music and dance, what have we left? If you don't take time to rejoice, you'll never truly find life, my child."

My eyes burned. I turned my back to the city and stared into the darkness. My heart reached forward, hoping, begging.

"Mama told me to be brave," I whispered, "but I'm not. I miss her."

Emyir wrapped her arms around me, pulling me close.

Months faded away as I kept visiting the city gates every morning and night. One day, as the sun rose in the east, dry air whipped up from the desert and cut against Palatiel's gates. I covered my mouth, straining my eyes to see down the road that led away from the mountain pass. A low rumbling filled the air. Swirls of sand crept across the land like a kaleidoscope rolling end over end. Mama had made one for me once, and the colors tumbled over and over themselves.

Wind whipped my face. "Emyir." I pointed forward, but she was already gazing that direction. The Torch Keeper took my hand and pulled me inside the gates. Her lips pressed together tightly.

"We must make sure every wanderer finds the way here. If someone doesn't see our light…" Emyir hesitated, and her jaw clenched tight as the sun reflected off her tan cheeks. "Will you guard the torch while I prepare a place for the refugees? The sandstorm will be here quickly."

I nodded as she hurried into the city. Turning my back towards the twists of streets and roads, I faced forward and positioned my feet in the rocks. The torch stood tall against the wind as a family huddled together and hurried toward the walls of Palatiel. I waved them into the city. Peering beyond, I saw other individuals pushing against the swirling air as they stumbled on the mountain road. My eyes caught sight of the torch.

Suddenly, the tempest crashed against me. I fell backwards against the city wall, and stone cut my arms. My chin snapped up and slammed hard. Sand sliced my eyes, blurred my vision. I reached forward and screamed for the people to hurry. My cry of warning was thrown into the wind.

Someone ran inside the gate within a gust of sand. Other figures became only shadows in the storm and seemed to fade further and further away. I shouted to them. Shoving away from the wall, I struggled toward the road but only found myself engulfed in tiny pieces of sand that cut like glass.

Then something grabbed me. I found myself pulled back into the city, but I tried to jerk away. The retreating figures were disappearing in the storm, and it was my fault. I had to save them!

"My child." Father's voice broke through the crashing wind. His strong hands clutched my arms.

"I have to go!" I screamed and twisted in his arms. "Emyir told me to keep watch. I'm a Torch Keeper; I can't give up!"

His voice softened. "You're not giving up. The King called you to be obedient, not reckless."

"No, I have to do more!" I lunged away, ignored his voice. My feet slipped on the rocks covered in a thin layer of sand, but I pushed forward. Out in the full gusts of wind, the world darkened as the storm blocked out the sun.

I strained my eyes. Gold light, sickly gold everywhere. It burned me, and I covered my face with my hands. Any person out there would be impossible for me to find now.

My arms and legs began to ache. Something like fire burned my muscles. Heat seared my throat, and it begged for water.

Water! I turned and hurried toward the gate before stopping short. Turning in a full circle, my mind began to spin. The gate had disappeared. Even the fire of the torch was gone. I dropped to my knees and crawled forward. Wind caught my hair and snapped it against my face like a whip.

I knelt against the ground, letting sand surround my knees. Sinking down, I raised my voice in a whisper.

"Father?"

No answer came.

My chin lowered to my chest, and I covered my face from the wind. Every move of my arms felt as if they were tied down by heavy weights. I struggled, then fell.

Something soft touched my hands. There was a strange cry, like a whimper. And then again, louder. Jerking, I forced my eyes open again.

Despite the stinging air, a dash of red caught my eye. I took a deep breath and convulsed in a coughing fit. Covering my nose with my dress, I tried to breathe again. Every breath of air stung my lungs.

But I pushed forward. The redness morphed into a shape. A round bundle lay in the sand, and I struggled to turn it around.

I saw two white cheeks inside the blanket. Rosy eyelids stayed closed, but the body shook with baby cries. I touched the smooth forehead with my burning hands. The child trembled against my fingertips like rippling water. Little hands rose, trying to find me.

The babe stilled as I lifted it in my arms. Tucking the child under a fold of my clothes, I struggled to rise. My legs fell back to the ground. I stumbled, tried to reach out for something to hold onto. All I found was sharp sand. Wind pressed me back to the ground, stealing my breath, and the burning sand seared my throat.

I held the baby tightly against my chest, feeling its coolness against my burning body. Squeezing my eyes shut, we hid from the world as the storm raged around us, burying my legs in sand. I tried to kick it off. Sand showered like a waterfall, choked me, and I shook as my lungs exploded in coughs.

And then a crash. Something dark fell. Light disappeared. The storm faded as blackness covered my vision. The last sound I heard was a baby's cry as my body sank into burning nothingness.

12

*beauty erased
in brokenness*

Something wet touched my forehead. I sank into a pillow and let the coolness run all over my body. My muscles cramped, but a strange emptiness settled over my mind. Silence surrounded me.

I pushed my eyelids open and stared at Ike's face. Creases lay around his mouth but erupted into smiles as he saw me.

"You're awake! I'm so glad." He pressed my hand in his. "Gamma told me I could be your nurse today. Do you want some water?"

I tried to croak out an answer, but my throat clasped together. Ike hurried out of the room and returned with a cup. Lifting it to my lips, I drank. My body sank back, exhaling as Ike settled beside me with a grin.

"You're brave, Kadira. I wish I was as brave as you."

My head shook, erupting my skull in sharp aches. I gritted my teeth but forced a tight smile.

"I'm not brave." I coughed. "I just had to—,"

"Save the baby? You're like a warrior, going into the storm to rescue someone! Father found you half-buried in sand and knocked right out where a tree branch fell on you from the wind, but you were still holding the baby and keeping her safe. That's super brave."

I tried to sit up. Ike hurried to prop me against a pillow so I could stare straight at his beaming face.

"Baby?"

He nodded. "She's so pretty, and Gamma said she could stay with us. The baby's mom died in the storm. It was really sad. The Torch Keeper found her, but it was too late." Ike paused to take a breath before his chattering went on even faster. "So the baby's got a new family! But you can pick her name because you found her." He hesitated with the smile lingering on his lips. "Do you have a name yet?"

I stared at Ike.

When I didn't answer, Ike hurried on in a low voice. "Because if you don't got a name, I have one. I think you should call her Nura. It means 'light,' and I like sunshine."

"Okay…" My forehead wrinkled.

"Oh good!" Ike scrambled off the bed and rushed to the other room with a yell. "Gamma, Gamma! Kadira picked a name!"

Nura. I smiled slightly. It did fit the baby.

"Oh, my girl!" Gamma ran into the room and knelt beside the bed. She pushed aside my hair and pressed her lips against my forehead. "We were so worried. Do you feel okay? Does anything hurt?"

I shrugged, wincing slightly. "I'm okay."

Gamma rushed around me, putting a wet towel on my forehead and offering me everything to eat or drink. But I sank back in the pillows. It felt as if someone sat in my head, pounding on my skull with a hammer. I groaned and turned my neck toward the open door.

Father stood there, watching us. Those eyes, blue like mine were supposed to be. They stared through mine as if judging my every thought. He smiled, but it wasn't real. Father's eyebrows tightened, and I saw behind the smile. I remembered how he grabbed me out of the storm, tried to keep me safe. And when I nearly died to save the baby, Ike said Father was the one to find me. If he did that for me, wasn't I brave for risking myself for others? Was he mad that I disobeyed his warnings?

I turned away and wondered how a hero could feel like a failure.

…

The babe lay in a cradle with a red blanket draped across her little body. I touched her hand, letting the tiny fingers wrap around my thumb. Each one looked like a flower petal, touched by an apricot-pink color. Her fingernails were like a drop of dew. They lay silent, so teensy-weensy and perfect.

Her eyes opened, and I pulled away. She stared up with cloudy-brown eyes as if she could see something I couldn't. When I slowly let myself lean into her line of vision, she didn't blink. Her body lay perfectly still.

"Nura," I said in a breath.

Her face lit up. Nura let out a soft coo and waved her hands. I smiled. Slowly, I slipped my hands under her warm body and lifted her onto my own lap.

The child never met my gaze, but her fists clenched and waved when she heard my voice. I pressed a kiss to her soft, golden hair and felt the heat from her body sweep over me. She leaned into my chest. Her heart pounded against mine. My breath caught.

Children rushed through the door, stomping their feet on the hard floor. I jerked away and slipped Nura back into the cradle. When my hands left her, Nura let out a cry.

"She's so cute!" Ike leaned over her and caressed her cheek with his dirty finger. Nura smiled again.

Another person came beside us. Faine shrugged and crossed his arms with a slight smirk. "Too bad she's never going to be normal."

I stiffened, but Ike stood and faced Faine. "What are you talking about?"

Faine turned his back on Nura. "She's a disabled orphan. How bad can it get?"

"She is beautiful." I shoved Faine away from the cradle and stood between them.

"Beautiful and blind."

His taunting laugh made my lips press together. I grabbed his collar and held on as tight as I could, twisting it to choke out his mocking smile. My legs kicked at him as I yelled in his face.

"She's perfect! You're lying!"

"Kadira!" Ike pulled me off Faine. Their faces flushed red.

"Sure, I'm lying," Faine glared at me with a sideways grin. "Gamma told me all about it. The baby couldn't defend herself from the storm. That's why her eyes are so light and blurry; the grit scratched them all up, and she'll never be able to see again. Talk about helpless." He jabbed a finger at me. "Your little, rescued baby should still be out there in the sand. It would have been better off for her."

Ike held me from beating up Faine right there, but my cheeks burned. As Faine disappeared out the door, I grabbed Ike and stared him in the face.

"He's lying, isn't he?"

Ike looked away. I jerked aside to kneel beside Nura. She opened and closed her mouth as she stared straight ahead into nothingness. Her pale brown eyes never met my gaze. They never hesitated, never blinked.

Ike pulled Nura into his arms and pressed his cheek against hers. His gaze turned to mine. "Kadira, it doesn't matter. She's just what you said—beautiful and perfect. I don't mind a bit if she's blind, 'cause she's still just a baby."

I nodded, but a lump grew in my throat. Nura wiggled and cooed in Ike's arms. I stood and stalked to the doorway.

To my left, I spotted the carpentry shop. Lights shone from its windows, and a figure moved inside. My heart leapt.

"I'll be right back," I called as I ran away from the house. Throwing open the shop door, I entered the dusty room and inhaled the smell of fresh wood carvings.

Father faced me. He smiled slightly and brushed a hand through his beard, creating a poof of dust. Before him lay a small, wooden doll that was beginning to smile in a half-carved face.

"I want you to teach me," I said. Grabbing his bow staff, I thrust it at him. Its smooth sides made my hands tingle. "I need to know how to fight."

He took it and gently twirled the staff. It spun like magic, obeying his fingers without command. When it stilled, his blue eyes cut toward mine.

"I'm a Torch Keeper," I said, fiddling with a crease of my dress. "Don't I need to know how to defend myself?" I remembered Faine, how his eyes flashed angry. I couldn't let him hurt Nura.

"One day. Soon."

I stiffened. "Why not now? I've been here for almost two years. I want to learn!"

He shook his head. "One day. You're not ready, my child."

I took a step backwards. Then another. My eyes burned, and I twisted away to run out of the shop before he could see the tears that threatened to fall.

I wondered if he remembered trying to keep me from running into the sandstorm. Maybe that was why Father wouldn't teach me. He wouldn't forgive me, even though everyone else said I was a hero. I wasn't good enough for him.

13

KAÐIRA

*from invisible light
to indiscernible questions*

Four years later...

Soft grass brushed my bare feet. Its tender fingers curled around my toes as I entered the glen and turned to scan the small clearing. With trees guarding the haunts, a stream bubbled through whispering grass. Flowers shot up by the edge of the creek. We came here often, but the simple beauty still made my breath catch in my throat. I released it slowly.

"Here, Nura." I took her hand in mine and led the girl toward a bush towering nearly as high as me. Together, I let her brush the dark leaves. A white blossom burst to light behind their foliage, and I brought Nura to where their fragrance slipped into the air.

"Careful," I said. "These are wild roses, and they do have thorns. Step here—yes like that—and do you feel them? Aren't they silky?"

Her pale eyes stared sightlessly into the sky. "What do they look like?"

"They're like—" I bit my lip and then knelt to her side. Lifting her face to the sun, our cheeks pressed together. "They're like the warmness that comes from the sky. They're white like the feeling you get when rain begins to fall on the trees, and we shake them, laughing, as they drizzle on our heads. And they're also like you. Do you remember? 'Nura' means light. The roses remind me of when you smile and your eyes shine."

"I almos' see 'em! Don't the flowers smell so good?"

"They do." I breathed the words for only her ears to hear. Taking her hand in mine, we followed the sounds of splashing water to where the others waded in the creek. Nura clung to me as we slipped across slick rocks and joined the laughing family.

"Roses are like rain, huh?" Faine jabbed me with his elbow. He rolled his eyes as he trudged through the field and sat alone at the edge of the trees, crossing his feet. I glared at his black shoes.

My lips pressed together. I pulled Nura onto my lap and held her close. She sank against my body as the sun washed over us, real light like the whiteness of the wild roses.

"Hey, Kadira, let me take Nura now." Ike stepped out of the water, drops falling from the hair on his legs. I looked up at his towering figure as an easy grin crossed his face. "I want to show her what the kids found."

"We're resting," I said. "The hike from the city was pretty long."

He took my hand and pulled it gently. "Come 'n. Don't you want to explore with us? Gamma put us in charge, and you really should join the rest of the kids. We're not *that* grown up, Kadira."

"I didn't say I was grown up," I shot back. I took a deep breath and pulled my arms close around Nura. "I just don't feel like it."

Ike nodded, but his shoulders fell slightly. Water swirled to his knees as he waded into the creek. The young girls and boys surrounded Ike as they raised wet hands to show their newest finds. One girl screamed when a boy put a slimy creature on her head, and Ike hurried to stop a mob from forming.

I turned my head and found Faine glaring at me. His short beard curled downward as he scowled. Then Nura touched my arm.

"'Dira, I'm hot. Can we sit someplace where 'ere isn't any sunshine?"

"Of course." My voice sounded harsher than I intended as I spun away from Faine. We slipped into the shadows of the forest where a soft bed of leaves sank under Nura's feet. She plopped onto them with a smile.

"What do you see, 'Dira?"

I lay beside her and stared at the canopy. She snuggled close as I let my eyes wander. "If you squint, the leaves turn to faint, green light with peeks of the sky bursting between them. Feel that wind?" I reached her hand up so she could touch the breeze. "That air shakes the leaves and makes them dance. It's like each one is a dancer twirling to a song. But here the shadows fall on us, making the world cool. That's what it looks like."

Her face softened. "Does it make you be happy? Like it's so pretty that no one could ever be mean 'cause it's a super happy place?"

"Kind of," I said, cringing, "but even beautiful things can't fix everything."

"But *I* 'fink it can fix everything." Her lips turned in a rosy smile, but I stared into her eyes. Those dusty eyes that saw nothing. They stared always up, never seeing my face. And I wondered if she would still trust me if she could see the memories and brokenness that surely stained my eyes like the moon-flower's drops.

Nura broke the silence with a big yawn. "I'm gonna take a rest. You can go play if you want to, 'cause I'll try to be brave by myself even if you're not wif' me." She paused. "But please don't go too far, 'Dira."

My throat ached, and I pressed a kiss against her cheek. "I won't. I'll always stay close to you to keep you safe. You're one of my favorite people, you know."

"I am?" She giggled, and color touched her cheeks.

"Of course you are, because..." I hesitated. My fingers touched her hair, but I couldn't say the words. Because she was the only one who couldn't see the person I was. The only person who accepted me. The only one who needed me, who would care if I left.

She smiled. Her lashes shut against her pale pink skin, and she lay silent in the leaves.

I swallowed hard and tiptoed away to where a tree stood with low-hanging branches. With both fists, I snapped off a stout stick and turned to make sure the sound didn't frighten Nura. She rested, closed eyelids toward the sky, and I brushed the edge of the stick between my palms. The smoothness made me nod, and I watched Nura in the shadows as I bent my knees and held the staff in both hands. Narrowing my eyes, I let the stick spin.

The stick cut through the air. It swung from hand to hand as my muscles tightened. With my arms extended, I rotated the stick from one side to another in a twirling circle that swept so quickly that my eyes only saw the blur of grey-brown. And then the circuit widened in a figure-eight. Sweeping from my left. Arching. A slice down from the right. Twirling, swinging. I never let my arms grow still as the weapon pummeled the air. Right. Left. Sharp twist. Jab.

The stick slipped, striking against my leg. I nearly cried out as I dropped the staff and brushed my hands against the aching, red skin. Grimacing, I pressed my lips together tightly and turned toward where Nura still slept. I had to keep practicing. For her.

Picking up the stick, I pointed it sharp to my right. With a flick, the movements began to make my arms move faster and faster.

A branch snapped behind me, and I cut the staff in a wide arc. Ike leapt backwards and fell against a tree, his eyes wide.

"Kadira!" Ike tore the bow staff out of my hands and cracked it against his knee. Ike threw it down onto the forest floor. "What in all of Érkeos do you think you're doing?"

My arms crossed, and I took a deep breath, staring at the canopy. "I'm practicing." I spat out the words. "Father won't teach me, so I'm teaching myself."

He grabbed my shoulder. "That's not the way."

"Then what is the way? Nura doesn't have anyone except me! Should I watch when others mock her? Who else will stand up for her?"

"No, Kadira. The bow staff is a weapon given us by the King. Father told us…"

I shook him away from me. "I don't care what Father tells us." The words stung, and Ike's face tightened. "I have to be ready. There's an enemy out there who destroyed my village, and I can't let that happen again."

"That was so many years ago." He shook his head, blinking hard. "They won't come to Palatiel. We're safe under the way of the King and his protection, Kadira."

"What if we're not?"

He didn't respond. Ike knelt to the ground and picked up the broken staff. He held the pieces before raising his eyes to mine.

"Please don't do this, Kadira." His eyes glistened, and he quickly turned away. "We're heading back home now."

Ike shoved the stick fragments into the soil and left.

I released my breath. Turning back, I raised Nura's sleeping body in my arms, and we found the trail down the mountain. Even the other children walked in silence as the sun set in crimson hues. Light burned behind us as we walked toward the east. I stared off into the desert's horizon and held Nura tighter to my chest, ignoring Faine as he walked behind me.

Palatiel rose, cutting the desert from view. The gates opened wide behind the dimming torch, and we entered. Stopping, I slipped Nura into Ike's arms and turned away without meeting his gaze. But he reached out, squeezed my hand. Then he left. The others followed, but Faine hesitated at the gates as Emyir appeared with an unlit torch in her hand.

"Stupid blue eyes," he hissed to me. "She thinks she can protect this entire city, but she can't. Torch Keepers are just pretend saviors in their heads."

I stared at him. My hand jerked to my own eyes and then stopped. He didn't know. He didn't see the color of my eyes, stained brown. But he saw Emyir's. My fists tightened, but Faine trotted away after the others, his dark shoes kicking up dust. I let out my breath through my teeth but tried to smile at Emyir as she joined my side.

"Ready?" she asked.

I turned my back towards the city and nodded.

Together, Emyir and I replaced the torch together without speaking. Somehow, we didn't need to say anything. Our gentle breathing in the evening air helped my shoulders relax. As we set the new, blue torch tall as a night guard, I straightened.

Emyir knelt and slipped an arm around my waist. I let my head tilt to rest on her shoulder. Her hair touched my cheek—soft. But I remembered Faine, and my stomach tightened.

"What troubles you?" Emyir whispered.

I blinked several times at the red sky above the desert. It burned my eyes. "Why do we do this?"

"Do what?"

I swallowed. "Every morning and night we replace the torches. Why? Mama and Daddy did it, and the King didn't keep them safe."

Her head leaned against mine. "Life isn't about being safe. If we worried about that, we'd miss out on all the adventures."

I looked at her.

"Our job," she said, "isn't to protect Palatiel from outside danger. We must protect it from within."

"How?"

She took my hand in hers. "Our people claim to follow the King's ways, but some are wavering. Safety isn't our goal— faithfulness is. We light the fire to show that this is a place where the King rules. That is why we must never fail. On the day we give in to the Prince's ways, that will be the day our cities fall."

I chewed on the edge of my cheek.

"Kadira," Emyir said, "people will resist our calling, for they resist our King. But he calls us to love anyway. And giving up is our decision."

I shook my head. "There are some people I can't love. They don't deserve it."

"That's true; they don't. But do any of us deserve the King's love?"

Standing taller, I crossed my arms. "Not Faine," I whispered.

She frowned. "No, he doesn't. But the King loves anyway. And so do I."

"How?" I asked, too loud. Ducking my head again, I lowered my voice. "He hates everyone. He's mean and ugly, and sometimes I want to slap him in the face."

She reached out and untwined my fingers that had somehow curled into a fist. Looking at my face, Emyir had tears in her eyes. "I love him because he's hurting," she said. "And because I remember. I remember finding a child by the gates one morning. I remember a slip of parchment, fastened to his shirt, with three words: *find a home*. He was bruised. Bleeding. And I remember him crying, because he did have a family—they just didn't need him. Something else was more important to them."

My hands fell to my side. "Oh." I stared out toward the road leading into the desert and imagined. And then I remembered. Mama. Leaving me. The tears.

"We weren't able to protect him from what happened," she said, shaking her head. "So now we try to love the way he was never loved in the past." Emyir stood. "Sometimes we love even through it hurts."

I nodded.

We walked back into the city. Closing the gates for the night, Emyir's eyes searched my face. Her forehead softened. "I'll see you in the morning as we light the torch again, Kadira."

I nodded, but the smile I plastered on my face felt stiff. "Of course," I said as I left.

Trudging home, I paused under the arch of flowers. Inhaling, I looked at the first stars. One began to move, slowly walking across the sky, and then dancing faster and faster as others joined in. Then footsteps sounded on gravel. I jerked.

Faine's shadow crossed near the corner of the house. I wanted to run to him, to say something. But I stood silent, watching as he hesitated and looked at the same stars I saw. I saw his shoulders fall.

And then he was gone, in the shadows of the backyard. I slipped inside the house. As Gamma tucked the children into their beds, I turned to my own room. Grabbing the door handle, I felt arms slip around me.

"Good night, my child," Father whispered, squeezing me in a hug.

I didn't answer. When his arms released, I fled into the darkness of my bedroom. The blankets lay wrinkled around Nura as she slept silently, and I pulled them over her shoulders. Blue light vanished as I blew out the lamp and slipped under the cold blankets beside her.

The night faded away in blackness.

As the first hues of morning light sifted into the room, I slipped into a coarse, green dress and glided to the mirror. Dipping my hands into the basin of water under the mirror, I washed my face and then rubbed my cheeks with a towel, shivering. My chin lifted. In the mirror, I stared at my eyes and raised the vial of drops. But I didn't put it in. I had used the moon-flower juice every day for the past years, as Mama had told me to do. Time passed so slowly. If Mama ever came to take me home now, I'd be as tall as her. Or maybe she wouldn't ever come back. Maybe she'd forgotten about me. Or didn't care.

I gazed in the mirror. Yesterday's drops were wearing off already. The brown stains in my eyes had faded to a deep blue color, reflecting the light. Their color pulled me back to the wild roses, whiteness shining pure when I was with Nura.

I looked down at the vial. Tracing its cold sides, I pushed it from hand to hand. The moon-flower juice flowed below the middle line of the bottle as I lifted it to my face. Hesitating, I set the bottle back down.

My eyes glittered blue. I shoved the vial behind the water basin and hurried to comb my hair away from my face. When I turned, I caught sight of the doodled pictures on the wall. Butterflies, flowers, trees, mountains. Scribbles of color. A little girl holding onto her mother.

I was older now, almost old enough to be a Torch Keeper all on my own. So why did I want to be little again and hold Mama's hand? She had told me to be brave. Was I not strong enough?

I secured my hair back with a clip and slipped into the early morning.

Only faint glows of gold escaped the night's hold. The streets were silent, and I let my bare feet trot down the cobblestones. I kept my eyes down, Mama's words ringing through my head. Blue eyes should be hidden. They were dangerous. I was right to hide my identity.

Maybe Mama knew I wasn't brave enough. Maybe that's why she never came back.

But a ray of sun fell across the street, and I quickly lifted my chin. Low, grey clouds let in a burst of light that warmed my face from the moist air.

"Little blue-eyes." A deep, yet gentle, voice made me turn. A man with jet-black hair and strong cheekbones smiled at me. "How pleasant to see something so lovely this early in the morning."

I blushed but kept my eyes glaring into his. "You're very forward, sir."

"And you're honest. I like that," he laughed.

I straightened. "Thank you." My voice dripped in sarcasm as I raised my eyebrows. "I'm afraid I shall be going now."

"Which is to my loss. It was delightful meeting such a fiery beauty." His eyes twinkled, and he gave a slight bow. "Have a charming morning, little blue-eyes."

I nodded and hurried down the street. At the edge of the square, I glanced behind me, but the man had disappeared. With a slight laugh, my cheeks grew warm. I shook the feeling away.

Emyir waited at the city gates, and together we lit the new torch that guarded the city.

14

Rekém

when a treasure too lofty
is all one can see

I leaned against the doorway of a merchant's shop, my back rubbing against the sign marked "closed." As the blue-eyed girl left the streets, I followed her with my gaze. She hesitated at the end of the road, looked back as if searching for me, and disappeared at the city gates.

I kicked up dirt as I hurried to follow her. My footprints melded together as the ground rose and fell in a collage of dusty earth. But as I turned the corner, the street was empty.

I ran down the street, turning from one side to the other. The girl was gone.

I stopped. I could keep searching, but why waste my time? I'd find her again. She couldn't hide long. I had all the years in Érkeos I needed, but if I moved too quickly, the people would become wary.

I rubbed the short stubble on my chin. The smell of sand and animal dung clung to the alleys, but I wandered down one anyway. Trash littered the ground. I kicked at a mud-caked can, and it rolled away clattering.

I slipped my thumbs in the fold of my belt and walked away. Under my tunic, the cold metal of my knife brushed against my skin. My feet pounded against the ground, soiled dirt sticking to my shoes, and every step made my knife jolt.

Ha! Two blue-eyed women in the same city! After all the years of wandering through the desert, I'd only found a handful of people stupid enough to follow the King. They were now gone, enemies to our cause no longer. But this mountain pass contained secret treasures. The gate-keeper and the blue-eyed girl. Two targets.

My mind quickly left the gate-keeper. She was a middle-aged woman, unbending in her beliefs and not much to look at. Most Torch Keepers were like her. But the girl…

I reached a fork in the alley and stopped. From here, I could see a green haze—the edge of the trees as they ascended the mountains. What would it look like from the clouds?

I could picture the blue-eyed girl. She would cling to my waist as we rode atop a flame-wing. The creature would bring us into the heavens where dew clung in the clouds. Ground dropped below us. Only whiteness. And I turned and saw the girl's face— those pure, blue eyes in a face flushed pink. A virgin who had never seen the world. Never touched evil.

But no, I couldn't ride on the wings of the air. Not anymore. I was a man; I would fight like one.

A window opened above my head, and a loud splash fell around me. I jumped away to see a woman closing her second-story window, bucket in hand. She never saw me.

My hair dripped, smelling strongly unpleasant. I cursed silently and wrung out my shirt. Water—or worse—fell against dirty cobblestones, and I shivered.

A bird began to sing a crisp tune, warbling as if calling to a lover. Chills rushed up my legs.

I'd killed other Torch Keepers, but this girl would be mine. I would take her to our camp, turn her to the Prince's side. We would fight and defeat the enemy together. And then I would sweep her away to the Sea. The girl and I would explore the pebbles of the beach where my Papa used to tell me stories. Maybe we would even find the Oasis Papa spoke of, and there we could live without the blood and war and anger. Me and her, together.

And Teion would be proud of me for turning the girl to his Liberation.

By the edge of a building, little white flowers grew. Pinched between the walls, they reached for the sky. My shadow fell upon them.

I plucked a single blossom. Its juice stained my hands brown, but its petals barely quivered.

Then I picked all the flowers. Each one fell at my touch. One white petal on the dirty ground. Another. Then another. They formed a collage of whiteness against deep brown. They were like the blue-eyed girl's pale skin against mine that was burnished from the desert sun.

As the sun began to rise high, my shadow disappeared beneath me. I wiped away drops of sweat from my forehead and turned to find shade from the midday heat. I crouched near the fallen petals. A door opened, rocks were kicked up, and a voice yelled.

"Get away, dog! No homeless on my doorstep!" A red-faced man raised a stick and waved it at me as I leapt away.

My chest burned, and I fingered my knife. A little blood would frighten away the blue-eyed girl and give me a reputation in this little city. My jaw tightened, but then I backed off. One day I wouldn't be the one running anymore. Glaring at the scorching sun, I let my legs take me down the street, away from the people who followed a King who took advantage of the poor. Like Papa. The King stole everything from him, from us.

The door slammed behind me. Slowly, I trudged up another street. Blisters on my feet ached as I turned a corner. Always walking.

A few clouds tumbled by and offered a lull from the heat for a minute or two. I watched the sky as I walked in circles and searched for something to fill my mind, somewhere to hide from the blistering temperature. How was I not used to the sun after all those years wandering in the desert? Maybe I was always made for the Sea—for the fresh, cool breeze that drifted in from across the water.

As I continued down another street, my feet left dust and touched crisp rock.

"Welcome, friend. Are you searching for a place of rest?"

My chin jerked up. From inside the doorway of a house, shadows met my eyes, but a glimmer of light shone through an arching trellis draped with flowers. Before me, a man towered, holding a stout stick in his right hand. As he waved me toward the crackling fire behind him, the aromas of soups and vegetables surrounded me. I looked up. The man's pale eyes wrinkled into a smile. A shadow covered them, but I could have sworn they were blue—blue like the fire, like the sky that let the sun burn my back, like the blue-eyed girl who had disappeared in the streets. Three blue-eyed dwellers in this mountain pass?

I inhaled quickly, but my chin tightened. I didn't need him. What did people think I was, a beggar?

"I have plans." I gave a curt nod and twisted away. The man's gaze lingered on my back as I let my feet lead me down a new street. With every step, I hoped to never see these people again. People who pretended to be kind but would chain others in their narrow beliefs, steal everything they could. The King's slaves. Like my father was.

Finally, noon crawled away, and darkness began to set in orange hues. As doors slammed and voices drifted to whispers, the shadows around my feet gave way to black nothingness. I let my feet wander like I used to fly through the clouds—not seeing yet not caring. The difference was that when I was flying in the heavens I was safe. Happy.

A light pierced the night. The city gates were still open, and two figures stood before it. They took the old torch down and began to light a new one. I watched their movements, quick like fluttering birds yet smooth and graceful. When the torch was burning strong, the two figures parted, the smaller person slipping away into the city behind me. The other person turned toward me, and I caught a glimpse of her face in pale, blue light.

"Torch Keeper?" I advanced with a bow. "I'm so pleased to make your acquaintance. Yet please forgive the time of night, as I am merely passing through."

She laughed, a silvery sound. Her hand squeezed mine before she pulled the gate half-way shut and stood by the side of it. The fragrance of lavender drifted around us. "How nice to meet you, young sir. I beg you not to leave the city in these late circumstances. I'm sure you can find a place to stay for the night." She motioned to her own little cabin. "I'd invite you in, but it wouldn't be proper, you know."

"I'd never dream of invading your home, m' lady," I declared with mock courtesy. My eyes met hers—brown against blue. "But may I ask about the blue-eyed girl who was here earlier? I'd like to speak with her on the morrow."

"Kadira? She was here just a moment ago. Are you a friend of hers?"

Kadira. I grabbed the word on my tongue and savored the sweetness it brought. The girl with pure eyes. The girl who looked straight into my face without wavering or turning away.

I jerked around to look behind me. The girl had gone, disappeared again. "Yes." I mumbled as I turned back into the city. "A friend."

The lady hesitated behind me, and then the gates closed with a solid slam. I could only think of Kadira. As a light mist began to fall, I ignored the drops and wandered on.

When a roof arched above the street, I settled against a brick wall and let my eyelids droop. A handful of stolen bread I had snagged the day before stilled my growling stomach while I watched the stars spin above me. Coolness drifted down from the mountains.

As night faded to a gentle morning, I let my dreams carry me above the clouds on the wings of the wind. And I promised to claim my prize before the girl could be captured by another. No matter what it took.

15

kaдira

countering unworthiness
with silent sobs

My chest rose and fell in a deep breath. I sank against my bed and let my knees slide to touch my chin. Coldness touched my fingers as I lifted the moon-flower vial before my eyes.

The glass felt smooth against my hands. I pulled it close and looked within its shadows, seeing the dark liquid drops that swished around the edges of the bottle. My eyes rose toward the mirror, where I caught their sturdy blue reflection piercing my own gaze.

What was wrong with me? Why did I have to cover up my life and pretend to be someone I wasn't?

My eyelids pressed closed tight. In the darkness, I remembered it all. Mama's last touch. Her words, "Be brave." And then her leaving.

She promised to come back. She said she loved me. But it was a lie.

My hands surrounded the vial in a crushing grip. I wasn't good enough for Mama. She tried to hide me behind the brown stains in my eyes, but it still didn't protect me. I was still a Torch Keeper like Daddy, still had his blue eyes. But maybe I wasn't brave enough.

I raised myself on unsteady legs. My throat burned as I tucked the vial in my pocket and walked through the house into the light. Sun shone through a misty, grey morning as my feet met rock, and my unstained eyes saw it all. Children's voices echoed in the backyard. But behind the canopy of flowers, I knelt on the soil.

And then I poured out the vial. The liquid spilled onto dry dirt. It stained. A splotch of red-brown remained visible after I buried the bottle under the vines and twisted my heel on the soil to pack it down. I turned away.

I didn't need to hide myself. My jaw tightened, and I tossed back my hair.

"'Dira, 'Dira!" Nura's excited call pulled me to the backyard.

I glanced behind me at the stained dirt and remembered Daddy's hands, giving me the gift those years ago. But it didn't mean anything. Not when he left me.

"Yeah?" I forced a smile.

The children crowded around Nura's tiny figure as I neared them. She stumbled to me, fumbled to find my hand.

"'Dira, here!" She raised her face to mine as if searching for my expression as she showed me her open palm.

I smiled and pulled her close. "You lost your first tooth?" The tiny, white tooth lay against her pale skin, and her face exploded in a grin.

"Ike pulled it out for me. It only hurt a teeny, tiny bit."

Ike drew near and knelt by Kadira's side. His wavy hair brushed Nura's as they touched noses with soft smiles. "Remember what we do with your first tooth?"

Her forehead wrinkled.

"Come." Ike drew her toward the middle of the yard. Other children gathered behind them as Ike and Nura stood with beaming faces.

"Now what?" She asked.

"Now," Ike said with a crooked grin, "now everyone must shut their eyes as you make a wish. And then you throw the tooth. If someone ever finds it, your wish will come true."

Nura's face exploded in a smile. The other children covered their eyes as Nura pulled her arm back and then released her treasure into the yard.

A dozen other children rushed forward yelling, trying to find the secret prize. Their voices made Nura stiffen, but she quickly let her shoulders relax and turned to me.

"'Dira?"

I let her hand find mine. Her cheeks were edged with pink as she pulled close.

"I wished—," her lips brushed my ear. "I wished we would always be a happy family. Is that a good wish?"

"It's perfect." I lifted her hand to touch my face so she could feel the smile I placed there.

Nura offered a big sigh and let Ike carry her away in his arms. But I stood still. The orphans laughed and ran, digging around to find the missing tooth. One child pulled two pieces of grass and held them to his mouth.

"See my fangs?" he said and began chasing the others as they collapsed in giggles and screams at his fake teeth. They raced around me, brushing my dress against my ankles.

But I shook my head and left the yard. My eyes raised above the city to where low clouds hung in the horizon. A slight glimmer of grey in the sky made my shoulders relax.

Little blue-eyes. A dimple touched my cheek at the memory of the man I met a few days past. I touched my wavy hair and played with the ends. He seemed so welcoming, so willing to just be a friend.

My feet carried me to the edge of the cobblestones. I stared down the street, light touching my face.

"Where are you going, my dear?" Gamma brushed my shoulder as she gently twisted me around to face her. She gasped. "Your eyes—?"

I took a step away from her, turning my eyes downward. Her gaze washed over me, her forehead knitted in concern. But I let my feet slip away.

"Emyir needs me." I threw the lie in her face and tore down the street. I could feel her watching my feet crash through the alley's mud, but I turned a quick corner. The words seemed to chase me, cut me.

They were *my* eyes. Why wasn't I enough for her? For my mama who abandoned me? I was nearly an adult. When could I finally make my own decisions? When could I give up the rules and expectations of others and be my own person?

The grey sky began to drizzle with a cold mist. Rain clung to my hair, soaking. Slowing to a walk, I swung my gaze upward and let the cold rain cut my face. Each drop burned. It blinded my vision.

Somehow this rain was different from the first one I met so many years ago. That day when I danced with Father on the cobblestones. This was hard, frozen. And Father was different now. He didn't hold me and love me like he used to.

A million thoughts rushed through my head, but I pushed them aside. I didn't need Father to understand. I didn't need anyone.

But I tripped and stumbled on a cobblestone. My knees stung, and water rushed down my dress in muddy streaks. A hand reached to help me up.

"Thank you, sir." I turned and saw the same tall man with black hair standing in the rain. His lips lifted in a slight smile as he nodded to me.

"My, it's not every day you run into a damsel half-soaked through." His dark eyes sparkled.

A breeze brushed me, and I tried to conceal a shiver. Instead, I offered a smirk. "Perhaps I could enjoy the moment if I wasn't the object of amusement."

He threw back his head with a rumbling laugh that made my own lips turn upward. The man shook his head. "You continue to amaze me, little blue-eyes. I apologize for my forwardness. I would offer my cloak as a respite from the elements, but I'm afraid it would do no good." He brushed his dripping cloak and instead took my elbow. "Yet I can lead you to a dry place if you would care to accompany me."

I let my face relax. "Of course."

The man took me quickly through the city square and toward the dancehall. The doors were already cracked open, and we slipped inside. A strip of carpet adorned the marble floors and muffled our footsteps as we stood, dripping, before the towering, crystal windows that glowed with the colors of the rainbow. At the end of a sweeping dancefloor, a dozen instruments of glass, bronze, and wood lay silently on a stage. The only music was the sound of rain pattering against the roof like rhythmic drums. I took in the scene and let out a sigh.

"I haven't been in a dancehall since..." My chest tightened, and I shook the memories away.

"Neither have I," the man said. His voice echoed against the cathedral ceilings towering above us. "Living as a nomad in the desert doesn't leave much room for celebration."

I looked up at his tanned face framed by black hair. "A nomad?"

"For so many years." He turned and glanced through the open doors at the empty square lined with rain. "I've been part of the Liberation since I was a child. Fighting for liberty against a cruel tyrant leaves no time for play." His eyes lowered to meet mine. "Or for meeting new friends."

"The Liberation? I've heard of it." Cold chills ran down my spine.

He shook his head, and drops fell from his hair. "Rumors, I assume. Our cause is often misinterpreted and twisted to frighten susceptible children."

"Then explain, please?" I took a step away from him and licked my lips.

"Of course. We fight for freedom; freedom from the King's strict ways in which he has imprisoned Érkeos. So many cities—like Palatiel—live thinking they are free. But really, the King has brainwashed his people to live a life in chains. There's so much more that can be attained when one is released from rules to live as he or she freely pleases."

I lifted my eyes to the stained-glass windows and thought of Father and the way I had to hide my own eyes. Color brushed my cheeks as I turned back to the man's deep yet melodic voice.

"We want to turn cities to the Prince."

"The Prince?"

He nodded. "He is the real ruler of Érkeos, and he desires peace. He wants children to be rescued from the streets. He doesn't want women to be tied down to home, not able to achieve their dreams." His voice rose. "Everyone deserves equality. Everyone deserves to use their bodies as they wish."

I nodded, but something pricked at the edge of my mind. "How do you know? How do you know your new order is different than ours? How do you know your Prince is real and desires more than what we have?"

Something like fire burned in his eyes. "Because I know the way of the King. I know how he banishes those who make mistakes. I know how he injures, he moves on, and he leaves his own people wallowing in fierce punishment." His fists clenched together. "I know the King, and he is ruthless. And I know our Prince offers another way." His gaze lowered to my eyes. "But so many serve a King they have never seen. Kadira, what has the King given you that you should follow him?"

I hesitated, swallowing hard. Memories of the darkness of night flashed in my mind, Mama leaving me alone in the empty streets. Jerking my head up, my eyes narrowed. "How do you know my name?"

Color reflected from the windows and fell across his face. His forehead softened. "I couldn't stop thinking about you after our first meeting. So I met the Torch Keeper, and she is very fond of you."

"Emyir," I said with a smile. I turned toward the street outside, where a glimmer of light seeped through the storm clouds. Glancing at the man, I nodded. "I should be getting back before they miss me."

"Of course." He took my hand for a second and held it tight. "Please consider what I told you, little blue-eyes. The Liberation needs more recruits. We need to bring freedom to this broken world, and one as gifted as you would be incredibly valued. I hope to see you again."

His fingers brought chills to my arms. My heart raced, and I quickly pulled away from his grasp. My cheeks warmed. "I'll look forward to that."

He pushed the door open wider, and I slipped into the city square. A rainbow's hue slashed open the sky as I turned with a small smile and curtseyed to the man.

He stepped forward and offered a last word. "If you ever have need of me, my name is Rekém. I look forward to that future meeting." He bowed slightly and left the city square.

I stared after him, my cheeks burning crimson. His words echoed in my head as the rain began to drizzle again.

What had the King done for me? And how did I know that he even existed?

Mud grabbed at my feet, digging between my toes, and I savored the squishing coolness it brought. But even that brought cold fingers of doubt. How could a loving King let my mama abandon me?

"Kadira, what's wrong? Are you okay?" Ike broke into the square and grabbed my hand, the same one Rekém had just released.

I stared at him and slowly shook my head. My voice caught in my throat.

"Come, let's go home." His eyes creased in worry as he pulled me through the city. Ike threw something warm around my shoulders, but my mind wavered behind me to the dancehall and the questions burning in my head.

16

Rekém

made for something more;
the mask that conceals

Every time I clenched and unclenched my fists, I thought of her. Kadira's hands, so soft and small in mine. The way her eyes washed over me, not knowing the dark secrets behind. Her smile.

I clasped my hands tight. With the rough city wall to my back, I let my gaze sweep down the road toward the desert. Where Teion waited. *No.* I ran a hand through my hair, letting a lock fall across my forehead, free. The desert awaited, not because of Teion but because the desert was where my future with Kadira would begin.

My foot pressed against the rocky sand. I jerked my neck toward the forest trees and bit my tongue.

She was there, gone up minutes ago with her group of peasant children. But they weren't like her. Their freshly scrubbed faces shone with silly grins and child laughter as they ran into the mountain foliage. Kadira was a princess.

I shoved against the stones at my back. Jerking my feet forward, my eyes trailed the footsteps she had left behind. As the sun rose straight overhead, I let the trees' shadows engulf me. A cool wind made my tunic swirl around my knees. I advanced slowly, pushing aside the stiff branches that tried to cut my face. This wilderness surrounded me, watching.

Something snapped, sharp.

I jerked. Twisting my neck to the left, I hurried forward toward the trunk of a large tree and pressed my body tight against the squiggled bark. It cut me, and I winced.

And then my breath caught.

Behind a thicket of brambles, Kadira danced. The orphans had disappeared, replaced by silent crowds of trees and toadstools that watched in awe. And I joined their ranks as she twisted her fist, a bow staff sweeping as if to cut the forest in half. Wind whooshed and shook nearby leaves.

Her elbow pulled tight to her side, and Kadira gripped the staff with both hands, tucking one end under her arm. In a sharp, circular movement, the stick swung from left to right, faster than my eyes could follow. So I watched her face.

Her chin stiffened, eyes sweeping the forest with her staff. A hardness settled over her smooth forehead, and her chest tensed without breathing. Every twist was mirrored by her body's turns and quivers, fighting an invisible enemy in a princess' dance. Round and round, from figure-eight motions to sharp jabs and twirling swings.

The stick relaxed. With quick gasps, her shoulders fell, and she inhaled deep. A smile lingered on Kadira's lips. She let the end of the staff meet the forest's leaves and tilted her head.

"Did I do well enough for you?" she asked, suddenly turning and grinning at me as light reflected off her face.

I inhaled quickly but stepped out, sauntering to lean against a tree near her. I shrugged. "Fairly well, little blue-eyes."

Her mouth dropped open. She thrust the staff at me and put her other hand on her hip, letting her weight shift. Her smile flashed. "Show me better."

I pushed against the tree and crossed my arms. "I beg your pardon," I said, licking my lips. "I wouldn't ever dream of out-mastering a beauty like yourself."

She rolled her eyes. "If you insist on stalking me, you could be at least a bit of fun."

"Stalking you?" I inwardly chided myself but instead raised both hands in jest. "Suppose I was. Would you be paranoid... or flattered?"

She hesitated, her gaze meeting mine. Her cheeks relaxed, smooth skin tinged with pink under the eyes that held me captive. The blueness glowing under arched eyebrows. Those lashes around the edges like lace. But the eyes, sapphire jewels in her face of ivory.

"I don't know," she whispered. Her eyes quickly dropped away. Color flushed her cheeks.

I studied her face, the curve of her jaw, the way her cheekbone accented the peachy skin. But she turned slightly, letting hair fall. It curled gently.

I swallowed.

"So." She gave a tight laugh and tossed her bow staff from one hand to the other. "You don't like my display of weaponry. Do you have a better option?" She avoided my gaze.

"I didn't say that." I countered. "But you have to admit—sticks are far too outdated."

Her eyebrows drew together tight.

I slipped a hand in my belt and pulled out one of my knives. "Would you duel?" I took the blade and held the hilt toward her.

She took it, the hard handle sinking into her palm. Kadira blinked several times as she lifted the blade to the sun's stray rays. "I don't know how."

"Try me." I pulled out another knife.

"What if I hurt you?"

I kept back a chuckle. "You won't."

Kadira shifted the knife from her right hand to her left. Averting my gaze, she exhaled.

With the speed of a sandstorm, Kadira rushed me. Her armed fist flew toward my shoulder. I side-stepped. She pulled up, twisted, and jerked the knife at me a second time. With every thrust, her face blossomed into a deeper pink, and a smile shone in her eyes.

Our blades met. Her eyes jerked to mine and then away as she slipped her knife out and swung an upper-hand slice. I deflected it and cut my own knife forward in my first offensive move.

Her eyes narrowed. As my knife neared her shoulder, she ducked, slammed her forearm against mine, and released thrashing cuts and slices that met my knife. Nearer and nearer, her knife flew toward mine, clashed, and pulled away like a snake, ready to pounce again. She smiled as she caught her breath and threw herself towards me.

I caught her wrist. Knives fell. Her body slammed against mine, and I clasped my arm around the silky dress draped around her waist.

A warmness connected us. I felt every heave of her chest, every pounding beat of her heart. She looked up. Her chin met my quivering muscles.

I held her close. There was no sound save her breath against my face as our bodies held together.

Kadira slowly pulled away. I released her, but my hands somehow snaked to wrap around hers.

"You did well." I whispered.

She blushed, and her eyelids fluttered. Slipping her hands out of mine, Kadira turned to grab both blades off the sod. She slipped them into my hands.

"You were easy on me." She laughed a little but then fell silent. Her body quivered as she took a step away from me, then another, finding her fallen staff and holding it close to her heaving chest. She tried to smile, but it shook her body. "I should go. Ike will be looking for me soon."

I nodded.

Kadira lingered at the edge of the trees. She looked back, and her eyes met mine like the last glimpse of color in a midnight sky. Her lips opened slightly and then closed.

I forced breath to move through my burning chest. "Thank you for sparring, little blue-eyes."

Color swept across her face. She laughed softly and turned away. Throwing her head over her shoulder, Kadira's eyes edged in laughing lines. "You'd better stop stalking me."

"I don't know if I could make myself." I smiled as I said it, but her shoulders rolled together in a little intake of air, the blush and smile mixing together as she slipped away.

I slid both knives into my belt, but my hands shook. Clasping them together, I tried to turn back to the forest and the city beyond. Yet as leaves changed to sand beneath my feet, I gritted my teeth.

Somehow, I still felt her little body near mine. And I missed it. Until I remembered: she was the enemy.

The sun set in darkness.

I shifted my weight from foot to foot. Before me, three shadowy figures lingered in the abandoned alleyway. My right hand rested on my knife, my other hand on the bag of coins in my belt.

"Only one woman?" A burly man swaggered closer. "Why can't you do it yourself?"

I took the knife and spun it between two fingers. "I gave you a proposal: thirty coins for her death. I pick the date and time. Is that enough for you?"

The men stepped back and spoke together quietly. I tightened my jaw. Every hair on my arms stood on end, but I stood up straight. I had to do this. To save Kadira.

They nodded. "Thirty coins. Paid in advance."

The edge of my lips turned up. I threw the bag of money against the closest man's chest, a younger guy who fumbled to catch it. A few coins fell, clattering. The man's short-bearded chin dropped and he glanced down at his black shoes as he hurried to grab the money.

"In advance. But if you don't show up…" I raised the knife and squinted at its silhouette against the stars.

"Name the time."

I turned half-way away. "The next sandstorm. And the victim," I swallowed, "the Torch Keeper."

They laughed, and I left them, my fists curling around the cold knife handle.

kaδira

something more, something deeper,
those limitations that drag her away and she can't let go

A thousand stars lined the sky like lights in a ballroom. I was the princess, with my night-dress sweeping around my ankles, my hair loose and falling across my ears, and my chin raised toward the sky. I took it all in. The stars shone like the blueness of my eyes. They sang their songs of the twilight. And yet, there in the heavens, they didn't hear the stinging words. They didn't care if they looked or talked or acted like everyone else. Each one was a jewel hanging on an invisible necklace—shining pendants.

And then they began to spin.

The stars shot from one side of the sky to the other, swirling, twirling. Two celestial beings met, revolved around each other, and then cut to opposite sides of the sky. The stars lined the horizon, dancing in slow circles. And the others joined them, every shining light becoming part of a silent orchestra of color.

But my chin lowered, and I looked down at my hands. Even in the darkness, I could see the nails, chipped and torn. I pulled at one and tossed the sliver onto the ground. My fingers curled into fists. And then I remembered how it felt when the tall man—Rekém—took my hand. How he held them gently. How he loved me the way I was.

The stars joined together and danced. But I wasn't like them.

My teeth ground together. I covered my face to push away the thoughts. Through my fingers, I saw another light burn into life.

I let my shoulders fall. Despite the midnight chill brushing my dress around my legs, a pale, blue light flickered from within the woodshop.

I found my feet brushing against the cold cobblestones. The light seemed to draw me forward. A candle in the window made the stars fade away.

As I drew near the door, a voice called me.

"Come, child."

I inhaled sharply yet released it through my teeth. Pulling the knobby door handle, I let the woodshop's light flood over me.

Father stood beside the three-tiering candles, his back toward me. He brushed a pile of dust, and it shivered to the ground like drops of gold.

I stiffened at his presence. Standing in the doorway, I pulled myself to my full height. But when he turned to look at me, he didn't seem to notice. He only smiled.

The door closed behind me with a quiet click. The smell of wood stained the air, and I scanned the room. On one workbench in the back, fresh slivers of wood chips brushed the area, and a handful of knives and chisels lay in disarray. I inhaled the dusty smell but stiffened my jaw.

"My child." When Father smiled, his eyes crinkled in wrinkles. He motioned for me to come closer, but I hesitated. The light faded from his eyes, but he grabbed something from the corner of the workshop. "Do you still want to learn?"

He threw a bow staff at me. I caught it. My fingertips brushed the slick sides, the way it fit perfectly in my hands. Setting it before me, the stick rose barely to my forehead. No marks marred its soft, wood sides.

But I stared into Father's deep blue eyes. My elbows tightened.

"Why now?" I asked, shaking my head. My eyes cut into his. "I've been here for so long, and you finally give me permission to learn?"

He clasped my shoulder. "It's time."

I averted my eyes, but I knew his gaze could see through the lies I hid behind. The façade. I never could be good enough. Not for him, for Gamma, for my mama who left me.

"I'm fine." I thrust the bow staff into his chest. "I don't want to learn now."

His eyes pulled tight around the edges. Father took the staff, held it in both hands, and found the perfect balance.

"My child, it is the weapon of those who follow the way of the King. One must learn to use it."

My jaw tightened. "When has the King done *anything* for me? Where was he when my village was burned? Where was he when Mama left me?" I stopped, feeling her own necklace around my throat. It made me feel like choking, and my voice lowered to a whisper. "Why should I care what the King wants?"

He touched my chin and raised it until I was forced to see his eyes. They sparkled blue, reflected in the glimmer of his tears. His forehead grew soft.

"My child, who was it that gave life when everything else was death?"

My eyes squeezed shut.

"My child." He knelt before me like he had so long ago. His fingers wrapped around my hand. "I love you. Did you forget? Forget that promise we made when you fit in my arms? That I would be your Father, hold you when you cry, and be there always for you?"

I shook my head slowly. "Things are different now."

"They don't have to be. I'm still willing to be a father."

I jerked away. My eyes flashed as I shoved my fists together and let angry tears cut my cheeks. "A true father doesn't hold his children back. He doesn't judge them and keep them from their purpose. A father lets them make their own beliefs and always supports them! He cares about them more than himself or his silly King."

He squeezed my shoulder. "No. A father—and a King—loves his children."

"Then the King should have done something!" I screamed. "He should have stopped all the pain in this horrible world!" I pushed him away and threw open the door. My back turned toward him, cold. "And you should have taught me sooner. I'm not interested in learning that weapon from you now."

I turned and left him there, standing with the bow staff he carved for me.

As the morning dawned in a quiet wind, I crept through the city gates and slipped onto the sandy stones of the mountain pass. Emyir's silhouette stood against the dusty glare of the desert. Her hair waved around her face as she stretched her neck to the air. I reached her side and paused, inhaling her faint, lavender scent.

"There's something on the breeze." She whispered. Her bright eyes caught mine, and they smiled. "But let us light the torch."

She stood back, her golden dress swinging free around her legs as she let me remove the old torch from its stand. I worked quickly, and the flame never quivered. It caught fast, burning strong as I lifted it back toward the sky. The old torch grew cold. I thrust it in the sand with a hiss.

Emyir's lips turned up in a tight smile. "Your parents would be proud."

I blinked several times but nodded.

"Kadira, I mean those words. They would be so proud. So very proud their young daughter is now serving the King and is faithful to her calling."

I swallowed hard. The lies slapped my face, but I let myself answer as if it was all part of me. As if the words were true. "Thank you."

Emyir took my hand in hers and faced me against the wind. We let the dry, crisp air cut our faces and play with our hair. My hair curled around my ears and shivered like dry leaves clinging to a dead branch.

"What do you sense?"

I lifted my eyes to hers, but they were shut tight. Light shone from her cheeks as she embraced the full gust.

I closed my own eyes. Inhaling the wind, a strange smell seemed to rest on the back of my tongue. The air whistled through my ears like a shrill bird's call. My eyebrows knitted.

"I'm not sure," I said.

"Mm?"

A dryness caught against my skin. I recoiled at the arid burn. Shivers ran down my arms as I opened my eyes wide. "It's a sandstorm."

She nodded and opened her eyes. "It is indeed. But praise the King that all are safe and well inside the city." Emyir reached for my fingers and entwined hers around mine. "Daughter, I will keep watch now. Go to your family and remain until all calms."

I hesitated. Her rough palms brushed mine. The torch still stood burning tall as I let my hands slip away and fall to my side. I turned and left her behind.

Inside the gates, I traversed the familiar paths. With only the pale, morning light, the city square sat nearly empty. A shadow flashed to my left, and I twisted around. It disappeared. I let out my breath.

Entering the city square, a familiar figure stood near the city well, but she turned toward me.

"Kadira, will you help me with this?" Gamma's shoulders slumped as she stood. Wrinkles marred her forehead, sunk through her cheeks to her mole.

I nodded and pulled up the vessel of water. It rested on my shoulder as we walked slowly back through the streets. Drops clung to my skin and dripped down my shirt, but my lips pressed together tight in silence.

Turning back through the city square, I eyed the dancehall. Its doors hung slightly open, and I imagined a flickering shadow brushing its corners. A blush crept across my face. Was Rekém somewhere watching us? Did he think about me?

"Ike told me you met a new man in the village the other day," Gamma said, and she reached to steady the water vessel as I stepped across the uneven ground.

I stilled the pot and nodded.

"Did you want to talk about him?"

I shrugged. "He's just a nice guy I met in the square."

"Is his city loyal to the way of the King?"

I kept my eyes staring straight ahead, but my cheeks burned. "Why would it matter? He lives in the desert. I don't think he has a city. It's not like I even know the guy that well, Gamma."

Her step faltered. "I'm sorry."

"It doesn't matter."

Stillness engulfed us as I opened the door for Gamma, and we both slipped inside. Father glanced at me, and strange lines creased around his eyes. I looked away. Placing the water on the table, I retreated to the corner where the children sat playing quietly. Each one held a pile of rocks, examining every pebble and its unique color. Faine wasn't there.

Nura found me and slipped close. Her body nearly filled my lap, but I pulled her close anyway.

"'Dira, these are my rocks." Her fist opened to reveal half a dozen colorful stones. "What do they look like?"

I touched one of the smooth objects. My lips touched her ear. "They all look different, but they are beautiful too. This one is yellow—like the warm sun, remember? And this one is like it but with more orange, like a soft, happy color."

"So they are happy and pretty?"

"Yes." I squeezed her. "All of them."

"Which is your favorite?"

I looked from one to another as I held them in the light. Each aura shone with its own color, dancing on Nura's palm.

"This one." I selected a pale pink. "It's the color of the flowers that grow, arching above the door. That's my favorite color."

"Mine too." She grabbed the rocks back in her fist but left the pink one behind.

"Here, you forgot it."

"No." She pushed back my hand with a huge grin. "It's for you."

I slipped the rock into my pocket as Nura found Ike's lap and left mine. A breath of cold air brushed my arms with her warm body gone. Nura and Ike rocked back and forth on the other side of the room. He threw back his head and laughed, Nura's giggling mixing with his.

She fit so perfectly in Ike's arms. He tickled and prodded her, and Nura responded with beaming smiles. When her sightless eyes turned toward his face, it was almost as if she could see the light of his smile.

The storm grew. A blast of air cut against the roof, and I stiffened as I watched the younger children continue their games. Yet my eyes kept turning back to Ike and Nura, sitting and laughing together across the room. So close yet so far away. It was like they didn't need me anymore.

Wind crashed and billowed. Something loud rapped against the roof, like an invisible fist pounding to get in. The children screamed and ran to huddle beside Gamma. She looked at me, and I averted my gaze. Shivering, I pulled my knees to my chest.

Light illuminated the room. Somehow, lightning joined the sandstorm's fury, drowning the world in bitter, orange light. I buried my face and tried to hide from it.

But it all came back.

Mama. Us riding through the desert. The explosions, the sand, the goodbyes that separated us forever.

My throat burned, and I inhaled quickly.

And then the door flew open. My face shot up. Rekém's hair curled in all directions, but his eyes stared at mine. Wild. Flashing. His lips pulled tight as air gushed around his body. Sand littered the doorway. Wind.

"Kadira." His voice came in gasps as his chest heaved. "The Torch Keeper. She told me to call you. A family disappeared in the storm, and you must help her find them."

I shot to my feet, the blood draining from my face. Running to him, I clutched his arm. My body began to shake amidst the tremor of the storm.

"Emyir? Is she out there now? Where did the family go?"

Another hand seized me and pulled me out of the wind, but I struggled away. Father's gaze deepened as he stood between me and Rekém. His head shook.

"You must remain, my child."

I looked over his shoulder and met Rekém's gaze. My face flushed hot as I glared at Father. "How could I remain when Emyir needs me? I'm not a child anymore!"

Father's forehead shattered. The pale blue in his eyes turned away as he released me and stepped back toward the fire. My eyes scanned the room, the children, the stares watching me. Every eye saw mine. Except Nura, still snuggling on Ike's lap.

I tore away from Father's gaze and let the storm pull me forward in its clutch.

18

KAÐIRA

sometimes life hurts, light fades;
they say it's okay, but it's not

Sand swirled around my legs like the fear climbing into my heart. I shook it off, but the grains cut. Burned. In the burning wind, sand singed like sparks from a fire. I couldn't breathe.

When I wavered, Rekém's arm tightened around my shoulders. We pushed into the wind, beyond the city gates. The ground lowered from the mountain as stones faded to desert sand. I lifted my chin, and my hair slashed at my eyes. Behind us, the last trees towered against the mountain pass. But then something else—a light. I squinted. Jerked towards it.

"The light, it's still burning!" I pulled toward the blue torch that somehow stood tall against the gale. We'd somehow passed the light. It was only a dot on the horizon, but the glow pulled at me. My heart lurched. My feet stumbled. If the light shone, Emyir must be near. She was still searching for the lost family.

"No, it's gone!" Rekém screamed above the howling wind. "The fire is out."

I blinked, tried to find it again. The wind hit me full in the face, trying to twist off the necklace I wore. I clawed at Rekém's arm to keep from being pulled away. My saliva grew thick, but I couldn't swallow it down. Dryness split my skin. Rekém turned me away from the city, and we pressed forward. I screamed for Emyir and the family caught in the storm, but no answer came. It was as if my words were torn away by the storm and shattered on the mountain rocks.

"Kadira!" A voice called me. I spun around. It was Emyir—it had to be! She was looking for me, not knowing I was safe with Rekém. The wind carried away her voice, but I leaned into it, searching.

Rekém pulled me into the desert, but I jerked away.

"Emyir needs me! What if she wanders into the storm searching for us and gets lost herself? We have to go back."

He shook his head and screamed over the sound of the wind. "It's just the storm playing with our senses. We must keep moving forward!"

"No, if the family is safe, she'll start looking for me," I argued, trying to hide my face from the grit as I searched the horizon. "I can't lead her out here."

Rekém stopped. "Kadira," he said, "right now you have to trust me."

I swallowed hard. My neck ached as I nodded, "Okay."

He took my arm. Sand stung my eyes as I twisted around to peer through the storm, clinging to Rekém. My feet sank into the ground with every step. A tear in my dress fluttered behind me, but I leaned my head against the tempest. Then silence. For a moment, my hair fell still, and I raised my eyes.

Clouds tumbled like an army, angry grey-green on the horizon. Across the desert, they fought their way toward the mountains and us. Lightning flashed, splitting the air with blinding light. I cried out, threw myself into Rekém's embrace. And then I fell.

With my feet, I felt something warm. A softness brushed against my fingers, and my eyes opened. There, half buried in sand, a slender figure in a golden dress. It smiled at me with a face partially hidden behind a mask of soft sand.

I shoved myself to my knees. Grit stuck to my skin like a million needles. But I knelt forward, brushed aside the dust.

Under the veil of sand, wisps of hair surrounded a bruised face. A cut swept across the figure's cheek and up to her forehead, blood dripping, drying on the desert floor. Sharp stones embraced the crimson drops. One stone, sharp as a knife, lay near her temple, stained red. The blood from the cut flowed out onto it like a fountain. I smelled lavender.

"Emyir?" I choked. Shaking, I threw my cheek against her lips, feeling for her gentle breath. But there was stillness. Nothing.

Her eyelids lay closed over pale, blue eyes. I jerked away from the peaceful stillness of death and lurched to my feet. My eyes rolled back as I covered my face with my hands.

Every muscle trembled. Recoiled.

My stomach lurched.

Emyir had called my name, but I couldn't save her. It was my fault; I had killed her. If only I had warned Emyir, called out louder, somehow sheltered her from the cutting rocks that stole her life away.

Dead. Gone. Like my parents.

The storm hit again. Sand and wind attacked me like a beast. Something hard sliced against my arm, and tears washed my cheeks. My chin buried in my chest as I hid from the world that wanted to swallow me in the quicksand as it had done to Emyir.

And yet I felt Rekém's arm guiding me through it. My mind burned with the picture I'd seen in the sand, the Torch Keeper who bled out on the ground, and I wished the wind would swallow me up forever.

I groaned. Sunlight pierced the air and pressed against my closed eyelids. When I rolled onto my stomach, something sharp cut my shoulder. I jerked, and my head began to throb wildly.

Strange shapes morphed like wind until they began to connect, whirling around me. As the world grew still, I found myself in a dome-shaped building only large enough to hold the mats thrust against a wall, a low hanging chandelier, and an empty rack of sorts. I pushed my own mat into the pile of others that were rolled tightly, and they bowled around in disarray. I scrambled to grab them. My knees hit hard rock, and I stumbled, falling on the mats and letting my body grow still. Pain shot through my body.

"At least you stopped them from rolling."

I sat up to see Rekém standing in an oval-shaped doorway, pointed at the top. He smiled as he leaned against the wall.

My face flushed hot as memories rushed in. I shoved them back with the bedrolls and tried to straighten my hair. My hands met a tangled rat's nest of curls.

"That was fully my intention," I shot back.

He lifted an eyebrow. "Ah yes, I'm sure, little blue-eyes."

I studied his face. Strong cheekbones lay under deep brown eyes that never left mine. His black hair was swept back and adorned by a thin circlet of gold, like a crown. I never saw it before. Was he royalty?

Rekém stooped to take my hand, and I noted the clean tunic, edged in needlework of green, that caressed his shoulders.

He pulled me up so that we stood eye to eye. I lowered my chin. "I—I'm sorry about yesterday," I began.

"Three days ago?"

My eyebrows shot up. "It's been so long?"

He nodded. "The storms to have stolen more of your energy than you thought. They typically do."

"Three days." I repeated, taking a step back into the room. My eyes caught on the chandelier above me, and I turned to study it. Its silver arches held nearly a dozen candles that shone with a piercing emerald color like the storm clouds that covered the world. The clouds that buried Emyir.

My body jerked. I blinked several times, and my eyes burned. Trying to keep my hands from shaking, I wrapped my arms around my body as I lifted my gaze to Rekém.

"What do I do now?" I stared beyond him to where light filtered through the narrow doorway. "I have... nothing."

Memories burned. *Emyir*. Death. Leaving Palatiel. And all of it was my fault. If only I had remained at home. Emyir would still be alive, because she wouldn't have been searching for me. My actions murdered her. I could have saved Emyir by turning back, but instead she was cut and killed by the flying rocks from the storm I had drawn her into. The family we'd looked for was probably safe, never knowing how they'd made us bleed.

And Father would hate me. Gamma would be aghast. Would they even care if I came back?

Rekém clasped my shoulder. "No, you have a mission. *We* have a mission, Kadira."

I let his hand rub my arm, and it created goosebumps down my spine. The memories made my stomach twist, but I pushed them away and let my eyes search his. Rekém's breath touched my face.

"We must secure the kingdom. The King has let these storms arise to frighten the people into remaining in their safe, little worlds. But we want more; we're the Liberation." He pulled me close and walked with me to the door. Sunlight dawned before us. "Kadira," he said, "we must not let others die like Emyir. We must let them dream big; have a chance to live."

Breath caught in my lungs as we stepped out of the doorway. In the daylight, the world exploded with life like an anthill. The desert was covered in little dome-shaped buildings where doors were thrown open and wind brushed through. A group of people marched past in perfect syncopation, hands empty and heads thrown back to the sky. Others paused their work to watch but quickly returned to their own activities.

Everywhere, colors flashed. Green, black, grey, gold. The sound of marching feet blended with a low-pitched instrument beating out the rhythm. And on the air, a faint aroma quivered like smoke.

"All of them?" I gasped.

"It's an army; what did you expect?" His eyes laughed at me, and we drew into the community. Beyond the dome houses, grasslands swept on forever. Sand and yellowed grass mixed across the ground, trampled by the armies spread before us. On our right, men on foot drilled with sharp knives, the blades flashing in unison as sun reflected on glowing metal.

I turned toward the left where stakes stood. Tied to each pole was a creature lying on its side, a black mass of leathery body. Their sides rose and fell with each breath, and even from the distance between us, I felt the rumbling of their snores.

"The flame-wings." Rekém's voice was only a whisper. "The wisest, most formidable creature in the kingdom. And to ride on one is like riding on the wings of the wind."

I gasped, "They're real! I never imagined." Jerking to stare into his face, I pointed at the great creatures. "Shall I...?"

He shook his head, and his eyes narrowed. "They are reserved only for children and weak women. But if an army of worthy persons rode atop their wings, what power one could behold."

Another voice joined in, this one low and mocking. "And what worthy men would be wasted who could have fought on the battlefield."

I spun around and caught the eye of a taller man with black hair like Rekém. A circlet of silver embedded with green stones adorned his head as he reached up and pushed back the bangs across his eyes. His arms bulged with unconcealed power as he elbowed Rekém and let his eyes trail freely over me.

"Ah, a beautiful girl you've brought me, brother. And I've heard she has spirit to match. A perfect pair."

I grabbed Rekém's arm. He tensed, but his voice came out low. "Kadira, this is Teion, the honorable Prince of Érkeos and leader of the Liberation's armies. And, unfortunately, my brother."

"Very unfortunate indeed." Teion threw back his head and let sunlight outline the sharp jaw that turned toward me. He rolled his shoulders back with a slight smile. "Welcome to the army, Kadira."

I nodded but kept my lips shut tight.

Teion twisted back to Rekém. "Make sure she's sworn in quickly. We have a battle tonight."

"I was just going to do that."

Teion gave the same stiff smile. "Indeed?" He took my hand and pressed his lips against it. When his eyes met mine, beads of sweat touched my forehead. The edges of his mouth raised slightly, making hard lines around his jaw. "I hope you enjoy your stay, blue-eyed one."

Rekém grabbed me and pulled me further into the camp. The paleness on his face was quickly replaced with burning red.

"Nice guy." I elbowed Rekém, but he only grunted. Chewing on the inside of my cheek, I let my gaze turn upward. "So, swearing me in? That's the next step?"

He didn't respond, but only led me into a low-roofed building. This one was rectangular in shape with a single fire burning in a circular pit, surrounded by stone, in the center of the room. The fire cast green shadows.

I stared at the flames, then at my hands. This wasn't the King's fire anymore. I was a Torch Keeper. I was a *traitor*.

Rekém motioned for me to kneel beside the fire, and I let my legs fall against the stones. They brushed against my knees. I wiped away the sweat that crept onto my skin.

Joining my side, Rekém's eyes flashed dark. His lips pressed together tightly as he took my hand in his.

"Are you prepared to swear your allegiance to the Prince, the ruler of the kingdom of Érkeos and leader of the Liberation?"

"Why," I gasped, "I haven't gone through this yet. What am I swearing to?"

His fingers grew cold. "You must swear your trust, your breath, your life to the Prince and his emerald fire. You must promise to live only to promote him and the freedom of the nation. Only then can the Liberation bring deliverance to a broken world."

When his eyes met mine, the familiar warmth touched my lips. I nodded.

"Swear it."

My tongue caught in my throat. His gaze made my heart beat wild. I turned to the emerald fire and whispered the words. "I swear allegiance to the Prince."

He nodded but ducked his head. A shadow fell across his face. "Then forgive me."

From the fire, Rekém lifted a glowing green shape. It wavered in the dusky air as his voice lowered. "Pull up your sleeve."

"Rekém," I began as I tried to pull away.

His arms gripped mine tight. "Do it!"

I reached for my shoulder, fingers stumbling. My face flushed as everything within me seemed to freeze. When my sleeve was up, I gripped Rekém's wrist.

"Please, don't."

His eyes didn't meet mine. Instead, he threw himself at me, let his nails dig into my skin. And then the burning metal touched my shoulder.

My skin became fire. I held back a scream as searing pain burned my flesh. My teeth clenched together tight. Tears cut my eyes. It was like a million needles stinging at once, like the hot sand that burned, yet I couldn't escape it. A sickly smell met my senses—my own skin burning. The scream escaped. I couldn't hold it back.

He pulled away, and I cradled my arm. It still burned hot, an ugly mar embedded in my skin. The burn swept across my shoulder in the shape of a flame of fire, standing tall. My body rocked back and forth as tears cut down my cheeks, and I tried to keep back the pain that burned nearer.

"I'm sorry." He wiped my tears away and squeezed my good arm. "But now you are forever one of us. Nothing can change that."

I looked through my blurry eyes and nodded. Yet the pain still throbbed with every breath I took, and I turned away from Rekém.

"Rest now, little blue-eyes." He pressed a kiss against my hair. "We have a battle to fight at twilight."

19

Rekém

*lost in bondage, every road
a threatening infinitude of nothingness*

My stomach churned as Kadira's wilting gaze caught my face. I dropped the branding iron back in the fire. Quivering overcame my hands. I tried to clasp them together, but their shaking made my fingers curl to fists. My mouth became dry.

She turned away. Hair fell over her face and blocked it from my view. Her shoulders shook—the ugly mar I created.

The burning smell seared my senses. Charred flesh, red and raw. Kadira was now mine, marked by my own touch. But why did I feel like I had broken her?

Her smooth shoulder was stained permanently. And I had destroyed it.

I covered my face and fled to the outside world. Sun beat on my neck. I looked at the endless expanse of desert and thought back to the forested mountains. The cool peace, shadowy greenness I had stolen Kadira from.

But one day I would give her so much more.

"Ah, brother," Teion swaggered towards me, flung an arm across my shoulders. "So you're back. How many years has it been? I'd almost given up on you."

I tossed my black hair away from my forehead. A circlet clung to my locks, and I raised my chin. "You asked me to grab hold of the blue-eyed ones of the King. One is in the tent." My voice lowered, and I dug my toe into the sand. Kadira's broken expression burned my vision. I stared at Teion. "Another one I killed in a sandstorm—a torch-keeper." I swallowed, remembering the woman's voice calling for help, trying to escape before my hired men murdered her. "And before them, I destroyed nearly half a dozen others."

He raised an eyebrow. "I'm impressed. Duly impressed indeed, Rekém. I believe after a time you'll be sent on similar missions. We have recruits scouting out the unconquered edges of the desert, and, in the future, we'll expand to liberate the Sea and the western mountains. But for now we have battle plans to discuss."

My chest warmed. I lowered my jaw, but my lips pressed tight. "Thank you for the affirmation. Yet I will remain here for a time. Kadira..."

"The blue-eyed traitor?"

I stiffened. "She's not a traitor. I merely showed her the truth, and she was enlightened to turn to our side."

"And betrayed her own King." Teion glared at me. "A wise decision, yet a dangerous move. Ones like that cannot be trusted."

I grabbed Teion's wrist and clenched my teeth. "She is under my protection; you may not touch her. I assure you she is trustworthy."

He laughed. "No worries, little brother. The girl's yours. But don't let her wander too far, or she might escape and get caught on another's hook. Beauties are never faithful." He smirked and sauntered off, throwing his last words into the wind. "I'll share details about the battle tonight when you're ready to listen. Lovesick one." He spat onto the sand while I fingered my knife and wondered why I was never good enough for him.

20

kαδιrα

she tried to hold it back,
but she could not

We crawled over the edge of a sand dune. With every twist of my arm, the pain in my shoulder exploded like a million fireflies escaping from a jar. I hesitated and watched a spider scurry across the sand. Spindly legs shivered as he disappeared behind the rocks. With a deep breath, my right arm twisted forward to drag me over the grainy ground, and I grunted.

"Shh." Rekém never looked at me, but he pointed his chin sharp toward the horizon. His dark brows pulled tight across his eyes.

My heart thundered. I stared at his midnight eyes, something hot twisting in my chest. Rekém had hurt me. How did I still love him?

Holding back a groan, I scrambled to his side. The desert swept below us, glowing orange in the twilight. And like a gem, a small village rose out of the dust. Sabbax deer wandered through thin grasses, led by herdsmen that were only specks on our horizon. Beyond them, the light of the blue torch guarded the city gates.

Rekém's fist closed around a handful of sand. His knuckles grew white. "So many imprisoned within those walls." His whisper broke, the Adam's apple on his neck pulling tight. "So many living and dying in meaningless lives."

Our eyes met. "But tonight, that will change."

The first stars appeared. As shadows grew longer across the dune, Rekém rose to stand tall against the sky. He clenched a sharp knife in his belt as he stared across the desert.

At the same moment, a hundred silhouettes exploded into the sky. The flame-wings cut through the air, riders only black mirages on their backs. They erupted in the air like vapor and began to climb higher until they were lost amid the growing darkness.

Rekém's gaze followed their ascent. When he finally turned toward me, his eyes reflected the green torches that followed close behind us.

"You will stay behind the army. It's safer," he said, straightening. "Do what is necessary."

Rekém disappeared, and I stood alone. Armies of matching silver and black pressed forward on each side of the dune around me, morphing into a unified mass that marched toward the village as it prepared to sleep. The sand muffled the footsteps of a thousand warriors.

And then behind them, women joined me on the sandbank. Someone thrust an emerald torch into my hand as we waited. Watched.

The fire warmed my face, and its green glow lit the ground beneath me. And then the world burst.

Flame-wings let out their terrible cries in decibels almost too terrible for my ears to bear. They flew above the city in streaks of blackness and flaming green wings. Flashes of light lit up the world. The ground exploded.

We ran.

All of us rushed across the sandy terrain, only hues of metallic grey in a thickening night. Every person, every torch, pressing forward.

Ground fell away. Eyes reflected fire. And at the city gates, the air burned with the smell of smoke and blood.

I hesitated, but the others rushed before me. The outside world grew colder. I faced the torch stand at the enemy's gates. It stood empty. No flame guarded the city.

With my back to the city, I scanned the desert. Darkness swept across like a thick blanket until flashes of light exploded the ground into bits of dust and rock. And then I remembered.

There was a little girl fleeing the city. She clutched a sabbax deer, buried her face in the scratchy hair. Her mother reached down and pulled her up, holding tight. But the world shattered around her. It burst in colors of deadly light. And the girl's life followed as she lost everything and was forced to live a life she never wanted.

I ran into the city. Tried to hide from my memories. But they kept following me.

Fire burned around me. It seared my eyes, and I covered my face with my hands. Wind whipped my hair back, sliced my cheeks.

Something wet sank around my foot. I tripped but pushed forward. Another street, another memory chasing me.

And then a shadow moved. I twisted away, nearly missing a thrust from a bow staff. The stick pulled back against the figure as he twirled it in quick circles, walking around me like a cat picking off its prey.

I cut to my right, but the staff smashed through my ribs. My body collapsed. I grabbed my shoulder, screamed at the pain that shot up.

My fingers touched metal, and I grabbed the knife Rekém had given me. With a twist, it left my hand and flew.

The staff fell to the ground, clattering. Panting hard, the figure fell against the stony ground and grew still. The knife protruded from his stomach.

I took a step back, but the man didn't move. Another step. Sand crunched under my feet.

My back hit a stone wall. I couldn't look anywhere else but forward.

I had killed a man.

And then another figure rushed at me. His bow staff swung toward my head, and I ducked. Without my knife, I lunged at the man's legs. We toppled. On the ground, I slammed a fist against his face. Something crunched.

As he rose, I twisted his staff out of his hand. Catching my breath, I slammed the stick against his chest. He screamed and scrambled to grab me.

I swung again, this time toward his head. And he didn't rise.

Screams erupted around me. Fire blasted through my lungs. I turned and ran. Someone grabbed my good arm. I swung around, my eyes flashing wild in the growing light. Rekém held his own knife and used it to motion toward the shadows.

"Get them. Bring them to the encampment."

I stared at his face. A strange pallor crossed under his dark eyes, and he gripped the knife in a tight fist, veins pressing ridges in his skin. Blood stained his knuckles. He looked at me. Behind his clenched jaw, lines marred his forehead as if every slash of his blade was another memory that remained embedded in his mind.

"Get them," he said again, his feet stumbling away from me. Shaking his head, he disappeared, crashing into the flickering darkness.

I wavered. My mouth pulled tight as I faltered forward. The shadows dimmed to reveal the faces of a dozen children.

I recoiled, but a little hand grasped mine. Pinched faces stained with tears looked up at my eyes, begged me for hope. A girl's little cheeks shook with every sob, like a mouse's whiskered face as it asks for only a chance to live.

I shook my head and tried to pull away. Who was I? I killed people. I shouldn't be here. I couldn't save them.

"Where's Ra-Mommy?" a voice asked.

Another girl grabbed me. "Od-Daddy said he'd come back. Did you see him?"

The children crowded closer and closer. Fingers reached for me.

I swallowed hard. What if I'd killed that father who would never return? The children's faces looked into mine—a million questions. My voice cracked, "I don't know." I stared off into the distant stars that dimmed in the glowing of fire. Something exploded nearby, and sparks flew high in the air. A baby began to scream, and another child thrust the infant into my arms. I looked down on the button nose and forced myself to think. "Children, come with me. Quickly now."

We hurried down the alleys, toward the city gates. Pattering feet followed mine through broken cobblestones. Tears faded in the growing wind. And then we left the town behind.

As we finally climbed the last desert dune, I strained my neck and saw the town going up in clouds of fire and smoke. The children grasped my legs as I led them to a future in the darkness.

…

A dim sun shone as I crossed the encampment, and the clouds matched the silver of my dress. Something rang high, and I paused to watch a man sharpen a knife. *The blade.* The death it brought.

My fists clenched until I could catch my breath again.

I let my gaze trail down to my shoulder. With the sleeveless dress that hung, draped against my collar bones, a scar cracked on my upper arm for the whole world to see. I tried to cover it with my hand, but the heat made it ache. A group of women passed, and everyone was the same.

We were marked. We were together.

But I sank against the sand and buried my face in my hands. We were the Liberation, rescuing villages from the King's ruthless hold. Then why did I feel so stained, so broken?

I killed two men. They could have been fathers.

My fingers dug in the sandy grit. I clenched until it burned. These worthless hands stole life. Who was I now?

The ground shifted beside me. "Little blue-eyes?"

I looked through burning eyes to see Rekém's dark hair falling loose under a circlet. He unwrapped my fingers from the desert ground and placed them around his own hand. Through the lines on his face, he offered a slight smile.

"I'm sorry," he said.

I didn't say anything. Couldn't say anything. My lips twisted as I hid my face from his.

"Kadira." He touched my chin and turned it toward him. "We're fighting to liberate this land. They need the Prince because my brother—even though he's sometimes harsh and detached—he sees a bigger purpose. He's going to revolutionize this land. But sometimes it's hard."

"Hard?" I blinked quickly and offered a tight laugh. "Like killing someone? That's just… hard?"

He pulled my fingers to his lips and pressed tight. When he released the kiss, my hand fell free. He stared off into the distance, and something clouded his face.

"I hate war." The words faded to a whisper, and he swallowed hard. His throat jerked. "I hate the killing and darkness and fear."

"Then why do you do it?"

He shook his head in tight jerks. "I don't know." Rekém ran a hand through his hair, and it caught on the circlet. He pulled it off and traced the metal band. "I don't know. I just hope this war will bring peace. Somehow. When Teion reigns, we'll finally be able to give up this hate and violence. It just looks so… distant."

A slight shudder ran through my body, and I wrapped my arms tight around me. Jerking to my feet, I left Rekém, ignoring his broken whisper as he called after me.

Could war bring peace? Or was this a façade we fell for, something that would never end? If we finally brought unity to Érkeos, would that justify the blood I shed?

I looked down at my fingers and cringed. Everyone killed. It was okay, because we fought to save.

But what if we were wrong?

Nearing the open fields, I crossed my arms and watched a group of children scattering across the grounds. A score of them regrouped in perfect lines, chins up and shoulders back. Following their leader, the young army marched forward, turned, and saluted.

They were orphans we saved. And they now had a home.

One girl had followed me from the burning city. Her eyes now trailed the leader, staring blankly ahead. Her chin quivered with each command, and she followed them perfectly. After the last set of instructions and the final salute, her face relaxed, and the children fled to the camp to find their noon meals.

The children's commander straightened. She brushed off her coat and threw her head back. The woman's eyes flashed, her crimson hair pulled into a tight bun at the nape of her neck. She walked toward me, then stopped.

My legs stiffened. I stared at her face, my own frozen in shock. "Ir-Ivah?"

The woman shook her head once, taking a step backward. She covered her face and fled.

"Ir-Ivah!" I tried to follow, but a million memories blinded me, flashing like the fire that had stolen my past life.

It was so long ago. Those days in the village with my family; when I played with my friends, never knowing life could become so bitter; those days I lost. But if Ir-Ivah was still alive...

I wandered back to camp, searching every face for a familiar one. But they turned away from mine and went on their own way.

Even Rekém was gone. I thought he needed me, but maybe saying "I'm sorry" was enough.

Because what was one life anyway? Why did it matter if I found my friend from childhood when we killed so many others? Life was a vapor. Here one moment, gone the next.

I had so many questions. Maybe Ir-Ivah had answers.

Behind one of the dome houses, I caught a whisper of red hair. Inhaling, I raced forward. Grabbed her shoulders. Twisted her around.

We stared wild into each other's eyes.

21

KADIRA

*when all she dreams of
is the shattered past*

Ice seemed to prick my fingers as I touched the smooth skin and scar on Ir-Ivah's shoulder. She yanked away. Her white face turned upward as she eyed my silvery dress.

"Ah, so Rekém finally found you? Kadira, his perfect, little prize." She tossed her head with a snort.

My hands fell to my side. "Found me?"

"Didn't you know? He's been searching for you Torch Keepers for years." Her hair fell around her shoulders in sharp edges as she shook her head. She laughed, stiff. "You have no idea, do you?"

"Ir-Ivah, please." I tried to reach for her hand, to hold it like we did so long ago, but she recoiled at my touch.

"Don't call me that." Her eyes narrowed.

"What?"

She shook her head. "I'm not that person anymore. Everything's changed. I'm my own person now, and I'll never go back to the simpleton I once was. I don't hide under my parent's name of 'Ir.' I'm stronger. *Ivah* is stronger."

My shoulders trembled. "I—Ivah, I don't understand. I wanted to see you. After all these years…"

"Oh yes, you wanted to see me after all this time. You perfect child," she snorted. "When will you move on?"

I took a step away and shook my head. "I just want to know what happened. I need to know. How can I move on from a past I never understood?"

"You don't have to understand to move on."

I paused. "Then why did you run from me?"

Ivah's lips twisted, but she quickly stiffened her forehead. Releasing her breath, she traced the flame-shaped scar on her shoulder. "It's not every day you see a friend you thought was dead."

"Dead?"

Her lips lifted in a slight smile. "My brother is dead. My parents, all that former life, dead. I moved on."

Breath escaped my lungs. "How? Why?"

"That night. I left it behind." Her voice grew low.

Something squeezed my body like cold chains, and I couldn't find air. My mouth opened, but no words came out. Instead, my fingers dug into my palms and pierced my calluses.

Ivah shrugged and let out a tight laugh. "Remember the celebration? I was so excited for the night's dance. I remember running to your house to find you, but you were gone. Instead, the gates were full of soldiers—our fathers—waving bow staffs and rushing into the desert. I tried to escape, running toward the dancehall where I thought you would be. I prayed I would find Am-Othniel, to understand what the commotion was about. But the hall was empty, and I only heard echoes. When I turned around to leave, there was green fire everywhere. And smoke, thick and horrible. I ran home. I cried for someone to help me, but I never found it. My house was on fire, burning higher than the city walls."

"No," I whispered. The darkness of the memories swept before me, and I strained my eyes to see through it. They met only shadows.

"And then I found my mother." She tossed her hair back and stared into the sky with a grimacing smile. "Slain, beside Ir-Haran. All my family, bleeding and dying from stab wounds. And I stood there. I couldn't say a word. I couldn't cry. I just looked at them as the fire fell and consumed their bodies. That's when Ir-Ivah died, and I became only Ivah. Braver and bolder and stronger than the former person I was."

I rubbed my cheek with a fist, but no tears fell. "I don't understand. How could the Liberation do this?"

"Oh, I'm glad of it," she said. "The village life held me back from my full potential and who I was meant to be."

I stared at her with wide eyes.

She laughed, "Of course, my parents didn't know that. How could they have? But even though it was traumatizing for me at that young age, I don't regret what happened. It was providence leading me to my destiny."

Something pulled tight in my stomach. I gulped down my words, but they came out anyway, in a broken whisper. "And my parents? Did they—?"

Ivah's chin turned downward sharp as she stared at me. Her lips pulled tight. "When the Liberation rescued the children, they brought me through the city gates. I never saw your father among the dead, although every warrior was slain. But there, near the torch…" she hesitated. Light cut reflections into her eyes.

"Ivah, I must know." I gasped out the words.

"I saw her—your mother," Ivah said. "She knelt before the torch, clasping it like a flickering hope. Her body was straining, and sweat poured from her face. She groaned, trying to save the fire and the child in her womb that was being born too early. Men with torches and knives rushed toward her blue torch." Ivah's eyes squeezed shut. "I heard a mangled scream. And then everything was darkness even in the dawn, as if the world itself recoiled from what had happened."

My arms clasped around my chest tight. I should cry. I should scream and run away from it all. But I only let my eyebrows rise, gazing into the sky—blind but searching.

"Mama." My throat tightened. "Why?"

Ivah pulled herself up and folded her arms. "It was for the best. We must move beyond the past, Kadira. We have to keep living or choose to end it all, not live with this continual questioning." She tightened her jaw. "This is our destiny, after all. We can't escape from it."

Her footsteps left me. Despite the sunlight, darkness sank its claws into me and dug deep.

Three years later...

The wind blew, another day in desert sand like the years that had passed. How long had I been in the camp already? The years limped by, one after the other. I was an adult now. Brave and strong like Mama wanted me to be.

I stood in the doorway of my cottage. Blistering sun burned my vision until I squinted, and I felt crow's feet line the corners of my eyes. The curls of my hair hung low by my waistline after so many seasons of growing free. I grabbed them, twisted them into a tight bun. Slight wisps of hair escaped and fell around my cheeks.

But as the sound of a trumpet called the armies together for practice, I ran to join a score of others who held knives in tight fists. We slashed and twisted as our leader demonstrated, every wrist turning as one formidable beast.

The cold handle turned my fingers stiff. I stared at the sun and tried to cut it with my knife. I could move beyond the past, kill it, and leave it bleeding. Dead.

My muscles quivered and pulled tight. The woman beside me stumbled, but we kept moving. Another person stepped forward in tune to the commander's word. We marched forward, and the sound of the fallen woman's screams soon grew silent.

Almost two dozen of us marched together. We aimed our knives straight ahead and pulled back our fists. Young boys set targets before us. Tension grew in my arm. I shivered, shut one eye. Our leader raised his hand. And then it dropped.

"Kadira!"

Nineteen knives hit the mark, but mine fell to the desert ground. I swung around with flashing eyes and met Rekém's gaze. When I saw him, my cheeks warmed strangely. He waved to me from across the field, but I picked up my knife and turned to the leader.

The commander paused, motioning for me to go meet Rekém. Somehow Rekém had special privileges as the brother of the Prince.

The other warriors laughed. Fire crawled up my neck as I left the field. Sand crept around my feet and burned. But I ignored their titters and hurried to Rekém's side. He took my hand, nodding behind him.

"I was called to get you."

"Oh, so you didn't just want to see me?" I grinned at him.

"Any other time, yes." He tucked my hair back, but his lips turned down. "Kadira, there's someone here to see you."

My eyebrows pulled together. I slipped the knife into my belt and stepped around Rekém, our fingers touching for a moment. And then I tossed my curls back and headed towards the camp.

My feet fell short.

A tall man stood a stone's throw away. His blue eyes met mine like the warmth of a candle, burning. He threw a stout stick to the ground and rushed forward.

I could only stand in the sand. The dry grains seeped away my energy, and I was captured. Trapped. And I couldn't escape.

"Father? What are you doing here?" My voice was muffled against his chest. He pulled me tight. Embraced me. Warmth rushed through my arms as he pressed his lips against my hair and whispered my name over and over again. Like I was a little girl again.

"Kadira, Kadira my child."

Rekém disappeared, and it was only Father. Him and me. Eyes that locked. Arms that swept around me. My heart throbbed.

"My child, how I've missed you." His hugs held me tight yet gentle.

I couldn't get away. Somehow, I didn't want to either.

22

Rekém

*giving up, letting go
even when it hurts*

She didn't look at me. As the man released his hug, he took her hands. Kadira's eyes stared into his, never leaving, never moving. Something fled from Kadira's face as her chin fell to her chest. As if she wanted to cry but didn't know how.

Heat rushed to my cheeks. I should save her, fight the man who wanted to steal her away. But I took a few steps backward. Sand dug into the soles of my sandals and became grit under my feet. I walked away from the man with the bow staff and abandoned Kadira.

Why had I let him into camp? He was the enemy. His eyes showed that clearly. But somehow, when his gaze pierced mine, I couldn't say a word. It was as if he saw under the mask I tried to hide behind. Hiding the fact that I wasn't a warrior. I wasn't strong enough, brave enough. I wanted to be a child again, to run away and climb into the skies on gliding mounts.

I looked up. A score of flame-wings lay on their sides with their wings raised over their faces. Their exposed, leathery bellies absorbed the sunshine. I reached out and rubbed the closest one under his jaw. He raised his chin for me to scratch, and his eyelids lowered half-way. A calming rumble brushed his throat.

Before I knew what I was doing, I found my legs wrapped around his abdomen. The flame-wing raised itself in a low crouch, muscles tensed. Waited. For that signal.

My heels hesitated. One nudge and we'd be free. We could slash through the sky, conquer battles, fly on the wings of the wind.

But I couldn't do it.

I slid off the smooth back. The flame-wing watched me with round, disappointed eyes. He turned away and treaded toward the others, his tail hanging low in the sand.

If only I was strong enough.

My hands by my side, lifeless. I kicked at a pile of the dried manure that was scattered across the ground. It flew like dust.

One day I'd be like that dust. I'd take Kadira and fly away to the Sea where cool breezes danced off the water. Where sand was a memory and the sun only a gentle star. Where I was free.

I stiffened when I found Teion watching me with a curved smile. He tossed his knife in the air, catching the blade between two fingers. It shone before him as he looked at his own reflection, brushed the black hair that curled over his forehead like mine, and dropped the knife back into his belt. His feet crunched against the ground.

"Dreaming again, brother?" he mocked, elbowing me.

My knees locked, and I stared at the ground. Dust.

"It seems as if you can't remember where the past belongs, does it? I can fix that." Teion kicked sand at the flame-wings, and the one nearest us ducked his head. My brother turned to me. "I'm sending you off."

"I don't want to go."

"You must." He raised an eyebrow. "I'll protect your precious woman while you're gone. Your Prince," he said, jabbing a finger at his chest, "is expanding his territory. You're to take a cohort of men to the Sea and gather the faithful. In a season, we will be needing them for a greater mission."

The words stung. I ignored the smell of his breath against my face and took a step closer. "I'm *not* going. You told me to leave the past. Why would you send me to the Sea?"

"This is your chance," he said. "Go visit what you lost and realize that it's gone. You're never going to have what we used to have. But you could make me proud." Teion's voice dropped, and our eyes met. "You've only got one life. What are you going to do with it? Let it waste away or achieve victory?"

I pulled away, stumbled. My face flushed. "When will I leave?"

He smiled. "At the beginning of the new year."

"Get me a cohort. I'll lead them."

"Good. And Rekém—," he said with a tight smirk, "Kadira is staying with me."

I didn't respond. The anger burning in my face made my chest hot. I swung away from Teion and kicked another pile of manure. It stuck to my foot, wet, stinking. Ignoring the rumbling of a flame-wing as it called for me, I wove through the camp. My jaw tightened. When Teion was lost from sight behind me, I paused behind a building and caught my breath as it clung to my throat.

The Sea. Home.

How could I leave the past behind? Or was this my chance to return to what I lost?

"If only I could bring her with me," I whispered, "then I'd never have to come back."

Because what else was there to come back to?

I left the camp and found Kadira, still standing with the blue-eyed man. Their backs were to me, and I wondered if she would even notice—even care when I left.

CRR.

23

ka∂ira

but He never gave up

I knew I should say something, feel something. But my body only grew numb as Father released me from his arms and took my hand in his.

I tried to pull away, but he held me gently. My gaze dropped. Sand kissed my toes.

"My child." He blinked several times, and his eyes glistened. "I have come to take you home."

"Home?" My shoulders fell, and I felt the heat of the scar that stained my skin. If only I could hide it, could keep him from seeing the twisted mark.

He pushed back the hair hanging around my face. "Come, child. I have searched the kingdom these years and found you. Come home with me."

His order made me stiffen. I clenched my jaw. "I already have a home."

Sunlight shone on the tearful lines that creased Father's face.

"I am happy here." I pushed aside the memories of death, the battles, the past. I only remembered Rekém, his hand against mine, our hearts beating together. My lips quivered. "I don't want to go back."

His thumb brushed the top of my knuckles. "My child," his lips parted, "you were made for more."

"More?" I laughed. "More than living at an orphanage in a city closed off from the rest of Érkeos? More than being stuck in a world of orders and trying to make myself good enough for you by hiding my eyes? What life was that?"

Father didn't speak. His fingers squeezed my hand tighter.

I spat out the words. "I have purpose here. I have friends. I won't live under the King's overruling ways that limit me to being nice and good like everyone else. Sometimes we're not perfect!"

"My child, I never asked you to be."

I jerked away from him. Inhaling, I caught myself from stumbling backwards, forced my face to hold together.

"I don't ask you to be perfect." The light reflecting on his face burned mine as his eyes searched deep. His voice lowered to a whisper like a breeze through the mountain trees—the trees I missed. "I ask you to come home."

I covered my mouth. My eyes squeezed shut, trying to block out the confusion and tears and questions. And then Father touched my hand, let his fingers sneak around mine.

My brain tumbled. There was a sandstorm cutting my thoughts in two, mixing them around and around, and I didn't

The Torch Keepers

know what to say. So instead, I slipped my hand out of his and let it fall to my side, cold.

"My child, you are so loved. When did you forget?" he asked. "The children miss you; I've waited and searched for so many years. And your friend Nura..."

He touched my shoulder. As Father brushed my scar, I recoiled. He didn't know what I'd done. He didn't know the people I'd killed; I wasn't the innocent child I used to be. My eyes flashed, but tears blurred my vision. "I can't go back."

He nodded, yet his shoulders trembled slightly. "As you wish. I would never force you, my child."

He turned and picked up his bow staff. Every plodding step he took led him farther away. He never looked back, never said goodbye. If he searched all Érkeos for me, why would he leave? It was a lie.

But I couldn't turn away. I only watched him walk further and further from me. I still felt his hug that pulled me tight. His words, "my child." Would I ever hear them again? Or were they a lie too?

When a shadow fell before me, I felt Rekém's gaze watching mine.

"Why did you let him in?" I sputtered in the wind, trying to blink the moisture from my eyes. "Why didn't you turn him away and leave me be?"

Rekém took a deep breath. "I don't know. When I saw his eyes, I couldn't speak. It was your decision."

A bug crawled across my foot, and I shook it away. Swallowing hard, my shoulders quivered. Rekém reached forward, and I walked into his arms. He held me.

195

As the afternoon sun waned to night's ebony skies, Rekém grasped my hand in his. We walked through the silhouettes of tents, rising like trees on the mountains. His fingers curled around mine. My arms relaxed.

"After you, little blue eyes," he said, standing before the tallest of the tents. Rekém pulled open the door flap, and we entered.

A sharp chill cut down my spine. Teion squatted in the center of the room where a map lay on a table. A handful of other generals surrounded him, all dressed in silvery-black. My face flushed.

"You're finally here, brother." Teion spat out the words. He jammed a finger against one of the black marks on the map. "Late for the most important meetings, as usual."

Rekém slipped an arm around my waist. His gaze shot towards Teion as he nodded towards the other army leaders. Rekém smirked. "No need to bore your men with complaints, sir."

Teion glared at us. Slowly releasing his breath, he motioned at one of the closest men. "Proceed."

The man traced Érkeos with his pointed thumbnail. "You, our honorable Prince, began the Liberation here." He pointed toward an eastern area of the desert. "Currently, our strongholds stand from the north to the south borders of the kingdom. Now is the time to expand."

Teion ran a hand through his hair, and his lips twisted. "Yes. Our current mission: reach the furthest ends of the desert. Once accomplished, we will liberate the coasts of the Sea and the western mountains themselves." He glanced at Rekém, and his jaw tightened. "But tonight we have a closer enemy." Teion traced a line from our camp to three cities toward the west. "These villages wait for our Liberation. They are under bondage to their silly King, whom we will crush. As we speak, three armies are being prepared to conquer them." He stood. "And as for the leaders of our raids," Teion's icy stare met mine, "Kadira and Rekém will lead the first."

I inhaled sharp. Rekém's arm tightened around my waist.

"Meet with your cohort on the north side of the camp. They're awaiting you." Teion's glare deepened. "And I expect you back, victorious, by dawn."

"Certainly." Rekém bowed.

"Kadira," Teion said, "before you go, can we meet at the head of camp?"

My heart hammered in my chest. "Of course." I swallowed, hoping my voice didn't shake as much as my chest. Rekém pulled me out into the darkness, and Teion's voice continued as we escaped.

Rekém grabbed me. "What's going on?"

"I don't know." I choked, covering my face. "I don't know why he needs me. I can't do this." I whispered.

Rekém stopped in the middle of the abandoned streets. Pulling me close, his breath brushed my face. He kissed my hair.

"Kadira, you're strong," he said. "I wouldn't pick another warrior to fight alongside."

I blushed, but the heat in my face quickly ran through my arms. I folded them across my chest and followed Rekém as he drew me to the camp where an army—our army—waited for us to lead them to victory. But near the head of the camp, we parted.

I walked alone and waited for the Prince.

#

they said she couldn't go back

I waited, shivering, in the darkness. The metallic grey dress on my shoulders hung heavy. Moving past it, my free hand traced the smooth line of the scar on my shoulder. It represented who I was. The strength I had.

A breath of air tickled my bare arm. I jerked my hand away. Somehow it reminded me of Father, the way he touched me— touched my scar and loved me anyway. But if he knew who I really was, he wouldn't love me. He couldn't.

"My dear," Teion said, his voice hissing from the darkness like a snake.

I tried to stand taller. Facing the Prince, I nodded.

He smiled. Walking nearer, I felt his hand rest on my shoulder and rub the scar I had just released. Shivers ran down into my fingertips.

He turned me to face him. I felt his breath on my cheeks.

"I won't make this long. You have a victory to achieve before dawn." He pressed his fingers deeper into my scar. "But you have a bigger purpose than this battle, blue-eyed one. Ever since you came into camp, I've known that. Your future is bigger than you know. Grander than you know."

"Thank you." I whispered, but my chest shook.

He raised my chin with a sharp finger. "I was raised to be Prince so many years ago. My master was a Prince himself, although weak and flippant for a ruler. He taught me much. And now I must teach you—not to be a Prince but to reach your full potential. To fight for me, to give liberation to this kingdom, to expand our power." He paused and gazed deep into my eyes. "You are a Torch Keeper."

I recoiled. "No, I'm not. I gave that up when I left the mountains."

He shook his head, smiling. "One's calling is never lost. And, Kadira, I need you as a Torch Keeper. I need the power you have."

The Prince took my arm. Walking together, I glanced down at our legs, moving in syncopation. Swallowing, I tried to keep my stomach from flipping inside out.

We stopped.

"Here," he said.

I looked up. My face paled. Before us was a torch, blue for the King. It stood taller than my shoulders, pointing up without flickering.

"How…? I don't understand," I faltered.

"Aye, but you shall." The Prince raised his chin, and blue light reflected off the circlet on his hair. "This fire once belonged to the King. He created it. And you know how to light the torch, do you not?"

I nodded. Immediately, Teion whispered a strange word, and a flash of wind cut out the flame out. Light vanished.

I felt the torch in my fingers. Without speaking, I knelt. Finding two smooth stones in the darkness, I snapped them together, and fire grew, bright blue.

"Ahh, a skill you have, blue-eyed one." Teion smiled. "Now change the fire's loyalty."

"What?"

"Make it shine our colors. Emerald. Green."

I shook my head. "I don't know how."

The Prince rose, taller. "One cannot create Liberation's fire from nothing. It comes only through altering that which the King has made." He knelt down on the sand. Finding a handful of black grit, Teion sprinkled it onto the torch.

The fire sparkled. Danced. And then the colors faded to blue-green. He added another pinch of powder, and it stained the flames a deep green.

Teion placed the torch on the stand again. "Kadira," he said, "you are a Torch Keeper, and this is your mission. Only you and I have power over the fires. Will you accept your calling?"

I breathed out.

He stepped closer. "There are people in the city you're attacking. They are under the King's overpowering rule, as you once were, not allowed to seek their own calling, to be who they want to be. Will you change that?"

I stared at the green fire. I was still a Torch Keeper, the powerful woman Mama wanted me to be. But now I had a purpose.

I nodded. "I'll light the fire."

25

Rekém

the name he could never forget,
never leave

Without speaking, Kadira joined my side. My chest expanded. I stood tall for her, for my princess with blue eyes, but her face hardened as she stared across the desert. Side by side. Me and her. Leading an army.

Somehow, it made my heart race.

I swallowed. "The meeting went well?" I asked, nodding behind us.

She ducked her chin. "Yeah. Teion just needed to show me some things."

I waited for her to say more, but she didn't. Slipping my arm around her waist, her head fell against my shoulder.

"Are you ready?" I asked.

She straightened. Her chin lay parallel to the horizon where a little city sat, twinkling blue for their King who would, this night, leave them to die. A shiver ran through Kadira, but her lips turned upward. "I was born for this."

Even in the starless night, I caught a glimpse of the faded blue in her eyes. They looked straight ahead, courageous. Strong. She faced her fear and came out a giant.

Somehow, the little girl I met in the mountain pass was becoming a warrior.

An army gathered behind us, and I raised a fist. The flame-wings tensed. Their grumbles caught in raspy throats as wings prepared for flight.

My fist fell.

The beasts exploded into the air. Two separate aviation armies, one shooting at each side of the city. And before us, spies were already in the city. We simply waited.

The flame-wings disappeared into night's shadows. They hovered above the city walls as we all watched.

Suddenly, the blue torch fell to nothingness. City gates opened, welcomed us in. And we ran forward. "For the Prince!" Our cry rang out.

The sky erupted with green flashes as the flame-wings and their riders exploded the world in fire. Before Kadira and I even got to the gates, smoke and ash hung heavy in the air. Our spies welcomed us at the city's entrance, every man and woman pulling out their knives and rushing forward.

But then the enemy came. Bow staffs and torches of blue cut the air. My men retreated.

Kadira advanced. I lunged for her, but she charged toward the city's torch where the enemy tried to light it again.

Explosions sounded. Light split the air. My eardrums rang.

Kadira grabbed the torch. Swinging her knife like a whirlwind, she sliced a man across the face, another in the chest. Her eyes darkened as she fought.

I shoved my way to her side. Our backs met. As one beast, we raised blood-stained knives toward the enemy.

A lean man swung his staff at my torso. I twisted, grabbed it, and used its end to slam him to the ground. Blood poured onto the crusty sand.

His comrades' faces darkened, and they charged. Four men surrounded me, sticks cutting from all sides. I released one knife into a man's chest, my other blade darting in and out between the staves. Warm blood stained my fingers.

Then my back grew cold.

My heart seemed to stop beating. I lunged forward, let my blade slice through the enemy, ignored their screams and bleeding bodies.

As they fell, I twisted around and searched the sand. The torch stood, burning emerald from Kadira's touch. But she was gone.

"No." I whispered, throwing myself through the mobs of knives and sticks. Darkness concealed the world, only broken by the occasional flickering of the torch—the green light that watched, laughed at the death we caused.

Wind whipped my hair. Something wet was flung across my face. I shoved it aside and ran.

And then I saw her.

Kadira crouched by the city wall. Her hair was thrown back, and a large cut bled across her forearm. A man rushed her, raising his staff to slam it against her skull.

My chest burned. I thrust myself forward, but two men cut before me. Breathless, I lunged to break their barrier, to save her. They caught my arms, drew back their weapons.

I stared over their shoulders at Kadira. She pulled back a fist and let her knife fly free. It shot toward the man's head. He ducked. The blade sank into the ground. Her face hardened as she crawled backwards, her back hitting the wall. Her body shook.

The man crashed his stick onto her shoulder. She screamed. Crumpling into a heap, her hands flew to cover her face. The staff hit her. Again. Again. With every slam against her broken body, she jerked, cried, screamed for help.

I shouted and sent an elbow toward my captor's chin. It hit, hard. He stumbled back, and the second man twisted to send his bow staff into my chest. I bowled over. Stars flew through the darkness. I couldn't breathe.

And then a flash. Flame wings shot by, exploding the enemy. My adversary glanced towards the light, and, ducking, I grabbed his legs. He fell, and I slid my knife into his body. Blood pooled.

When I looked up, the world stopped. Kadira's assailant had disappeared, and she lay, silent, a heap of blood. Her fists were clasped against her chest.

I ran toward her. My body flushed hot as I fell to the ground and pushed her hair from her face.

"Kadira?" I asked, choking. "Little blue-eyes?"

She looked at me, tears staining her face. Every breath made her chest rattle, shaking the necklace that hung between her collarbones. She raised a weak hand, and I lifted her in my arms. Her lips broke open in a cry.

"I'll get you out of here," I promised.

Her shoulders shook. She sank her face in my shoulder as I stood. But then Kadira pulled away.

"No," she whispered. "You have to leave me. Go. Kill them all."

My forehead creased. I stared into her eyes and recoiled. They were blue-grey. And slowly, as the world exploded in our emerald fire, green seemed to seep into her irises.

Kadira's lips parted, blood staining them. "Make our Prince proud. We have to win this battle. We have to kill every single man."

I shook my head, trying to avoid her dull eyes. Trying to see the princess she was, not this hard warrior before me. "I don't care about the battle. I just need you. Safe."

Her body shook in my arms.

I wiped away the smudge of blood and sweat that clung to her hair. My chest tightened.

Her eyes began to close.

"Kadira," I pulled her to my chest, her heart beating against mine. Gently, I pressed my lips to her hair. "I love you."

Tears fell from her cheeks, and she grabbed me. As her breaths grew tauter, she held my cloak tight. "Please don't leave me."

I kissed her again. Stumbling, I pulled us out of the battle, the fire, the smoke.

26

KADIRA

stay with her,
and please never forget

Inhale deep. I winced. With every breath, the burning in my chest grew. I sank against my bedroll and tried to hide from it.

Yet with my eyes closed, it all rushed back. The darkness. The night. The men who claimed to serve a loving King yet attacked me. Grabbed me. Beat me. Smirked with twisted faces the entire time.

I gasped and flung a hand toward my neck. Breathless, I wiggled and tried to sit up. The memories burned. And today I should have been celebrating a new year.

But it was all different now. I had lit the torch. I had created green fire.

Shadows danced in the corners of the room. I reached for my knife's silver blade and the flint beside it. My calloused fingers scraped down the blade, tested it, and I shook my head. The rhythmic purr of stone against metal created a lullaby that made the chandelier's candles above me flicker in hues of jade.

The candles reminded me of Father. Of the dancehall that would be lit up in a million lights for the new year celebration. Ike would be there with Nura, everyone dancing and singing and celebrating.

My throat ached.

"Always busy?" Rekém appeared in the doorway. He entered the room, sinking down by my side and reaching for the knife. Nodding, he felt for the sharpness. "Nice touch you've done here, my little blue-eyes. Almost as good as me."

I elbowed him, forced a laugh. "I'm that bad?"

He laughed. Smile lines brushed by his lips as he looked down on me and drew me close to his side, carefully touching the bandage on my arm. "Are you okay?"

"Yeah." I lied.

Rekém let out his breath. "Good." He reached a hand across my shoulders and massaged, gently. Chills ran down my spine. Letting my eyelids close half-way, I exhaled.

"I—," he stopped and let his hand fall. He looked away. "I have dismal news to share."

A sarcastic retort caught on my tongue until I saw his face. A shadow crossed between my vision and the candles above. My chest burned.

"I've been stationed to lead a coalition to the eastern Sea. We'll be scoping out the land, searching for those faithful to our cause."

"But you won't be back for several months." My body clenched. I tried to breathe, but it didn't come. All those memories rushed back, and I grasped his hand in mine.

Rekém sighed, "Exactly." He released my hand.

I lifted my fingers to the light and bit at a hangnail, averting my gaze. "And I'm not invited?"

He stopped me, touched my chin and raised it to his eye level. A smile hinted by his mouth. "You've been an excellent part of the desert Liberation here these past years," he said. "We can't let you switch locations just yet."

I swallowed, hard. "Or you don't trust me enough?"

His smile faded slightly. "Some might not. But you know I do."

I let out a quick breath between my teeth.

"I'll be back before you know it, little blue..." He stopped and averted his gaze. Swallowing, he tried to smile as he tucked back a curl that fell across my forehead. "Just don't let any other lucky guy catch your heart."

I crossed my arms. "Don't mock me."

"I'd never dream of it." He kissed the top of my hair. Every muscle in my body grew warm. His breath brushed against my cheek.

"I'll be waiting." My lips parted, but he disappeared into the night. I wanted to scream to him, to beg him to never leave me. To tell him that I was scared and alone and hurt with every breath I took.

With my hands empty, I shoved them together, clasped tight. Grime stuck under my nails, but I hid them in clenched fists. My eyes roamed through the room, yet my face turned away. Two other women wandered into the room and prepared their bedrolls.

My breath constricted. The scent of smoke stained the air from the open door. Fires grew low from the dinner meal, but I was stuck here, in this black hole where my body hurt like my heart.

Months without him. I tried not to cry.

A week later, I stared at the sky and tried to count the stars. My finger traced a constellation, eight stars shaped as a torch. At the bottom, my hands dropped back to my side.

Another constellation, the Flame-wing, swept high above me. I squinted at it and tried to match up the stars. They seemed to blink, there for a moment and gone the next.

Something brushed my foot, and I leapt backwards. A black creature scurried into the desert. Sharp legs made rasping noises in the sand even when the figure was gone from sight. I pressed a fist to my chest and took a shaky breath. And then the pain returned, aching from the beating of the week before. I clenched my teeth.

And then I tilted my head to the side. Glancing at the invisible creatures in the shadows, I released my breath.

The stars still twinkled, but I turned towards the night. I trotted through the clutter of dome-shaped houses until I found the largest one. Light still flickered from within, and I took a deep breath, shoving aside the door.

A man turned toward me. Deep eyes glared from a head of dark hair, neatly combed, as Teion studied my face in the candlelight.

"Ah, my dear." He motioned to the center of the room where a table stood. Tender fruits lay arranged on fine dishes, and I inhaled their sugar-smell. Near them, patterns of imported porcelain complimented the violet flesh of berries and tender sprouts adorning them. Teion sat beside the table and offered me the seat opposite him.

I forced myself to take it, managing a slight smile for the man in front of me.

"Mourning the loss of your lover, yes?" The Prince slipped a berry onto his tongue, and red liquid spilled out. He wiped his chin with a white cloth. "My brother was needed elsewhere. I am certain I can find entertainment for your affection during this abyss."

I pushed down the heat that burned my face. My cheeks lifted slightly. "You are so kind. Unfortunately, you misinterpret my errand."

"I do?" He raised a glass of thick liquid to his lips, sipping loudly. "Then enlighten me, my dear."

"I want," I hesitated, "a promotion."

He set his glass down. "Indeed?"

My eyes glared dark. "If I am fighting for the freedom of this nation, I must do more. I can lead men, spy out a city, fly on the flame-wings. You taught me how to light the Liberation's fire. I can do more."

"Ah, it is good to fill in the void of a broken heart with busywork." Teion pushed a platter toward me. "We'll see how good you are. Return here tomorrow at twilight."

I nodded. Grabbing a waxy-textured fruit, I stood and turned to the doorway. "I'll be here."

When the door closed between us, I let my teeth sink into the fruit. It melted on my tongue in sugary juice that raced through my throat. I sucked it all in, my eyes turning up towards the stars.

Rekém would come back, and he would be proud of me.

I went to my tent. The stars changed to light as I slept, but the day also slipped by quickly. Another day passed. And I never saw Rekém. Maybe he was gone already. Or maybe he didn't want to hurt me more by saying goodbye. I still missed him.

As the next twilight appeared, I dug through a bundle of clothes in the corner. My metallic grey dress met my skin like silk, but another garment caught my eye.

I lifted the dress I wore on the first day I arrived in the camp. It was nearly the color of sand after all these years. I brushed it against my nose. Faintly, the fragrance of flowers and dust met my senses, and I pulled the cloth away before I could let the memories burn my mind. As I shoved the dress back into the corner, something fell out of the pocket.

A pebble.

I raised it to the light. Breath caught in my throat. The pink rock glittered, and I let it fall in my palm.

It was rosy, like Nura. I could almost see her blind eyes searching for mine, hear her words, "It's for you." Her name meant "light," and, somehow, I missed the light of her smile that never saw my brokenness. That trusted me despite my fear.

But I dropped the rock into my pocket and slipped on the grey dress. It fell around my body, fitting my form snugly without touching my shoulders where the scar shone.

The past was gone. I had to move on. But the pebble still lay heavy in my pocket.

Dusk concealed me as I stole through the encampment. At the entrance of Teion's dwelling, I hesitated. My eyes searched for the stars, but they were hidden behind twilight clouds.

"Enter." A voice hissed.

I drew into the building. The table was covered with a crisp map over which a dozen figures leaned over. Most of them were generals or leaders of the army, but I caught sight of Ivah's downcast gaze as she quickly turned away, her crimson hair blocking her face.

Teion pointed at a spot on the map not far from our own position. "Our mission tonight is simple. The city of Zircon is in an uncertain position regarding loyalty. They waver between our cause and the rebel King." He spat on the ground, and I jumped. "As you well know, the Torch Keeper's position determines the city's loyalty. Tonight, we target a single loyalty."

The others nodded. My shoulders squeezed between two taller men so I could see the map more clearly.

"Determine the Torch Keeper's allegiance. If he is faithful to our cause, he is our entry to the city. If not," Teion stared directly at me, "you know what to do."

I felt for the knife in my belt and nodded. A cold mist seemed to cling to my forehead, but I forced my jaw to relax.

A general nodded. "We ride for our Prince."

"For our Prince," we echoed.

The men crept out of the room, but I grabbed Ivah's cloak. Her eyes turned toward me, nearly ebony but with a hint of something else.

I held her back. "Ivah, what's wrong?"

Her cheekbones hardened, and she stared at me, wild. "I'm going to win. I'll win even if it means escaping from all this."

"Ivah, what do you mean? Please, you can't..." I reached out to her, but she recoiled like a serpent.

She reached to rub her collarbone. A wisp of hair cut across her face as she tightened her jaw. "Nothing matters anymore, Kadira." She pulled away. "We have to go."

I followed the shadows as they slipped through the desert. Quickening to a fast trot, the ground passed beneath us. I tried to catch Ivah's gaze, but she ran before me, always looking straight ahead. My lungs grew tight.

I turned around a cactus and stumbled. A man beside me cursed under his breath as my hands fell against hard stone. He ran past me, kicking up sand. I pulled in a sharp breath. Something wet and sticky clung to my fingers, but I raced to join the others, ignoring the way my muscles throbbed.

The leader slowed. We knelt to the ground and crawled forward. Hours seemed to pass. My legs ached from the sand's scratches, but I forced my breathing to become quiet. And then, finally, I looked up.

A town rose out of the sand. Before it, the torch's fire flickered deep blue.

We sat, crouching. Muscles ached in my arms, but I waited. Time passed. Sand blew in my face. And then the gate opened.

A figure walked toward the torch and took down the old one whose flame that grew low. He shoved it in the sand then stood to raise a new one into place.

We attacked.

Within seconds, the man was pulled away from the torch. The blue fire went out. I lit the torch again, sprinkling black powder into the blueness to stain it green. It grew tall, illuminated Érkeos for our Liberation. The fire cast light onto the man's face as he was quickly surrounded by our warriors. His eyes met my face, and I averted my gaze to avoid his pure, blue eyes.

Our leader stepped forward. "State your allegiance to the Prince and live."

The man lifted his chin, a beard framing his small face. His eyes shone beady yet bright as his lips parted in quick pants. Our warriors forced him to his knees, and he hit the ground with a groan but never cried out.

"Your allegiance!" The leader struck him across the face, leaving a bleeding gash.

The man smiled slightly. "I follow the way of the King, and I will only live for him."

I stepped back as the leader's face exploded in a widening grin. "Ah, innocent mind. What you will pay for those words."

I followed the group as they dragged the man into the city. Someone grabbed the torch, took it with us. At the gate, a tiny cabin appeared. Only a thatched roof adorned the one-window home, and wooden walls stood like sentries about to fall.

"Uriel?" A woman stepped out of the cabin and blinked in the green light. "My husband?"

The man tried to throw himself forward, but the guards held him. They struck him with the hilt of their daggers, and he collapsed onto the ground with a groan.

"My pardons, Madam," our leader said as he caressed a lock of her hair for a moment. "Your husband has made some bad life choices. I'm afraid it affects you and your family as well."

Her shoulders pushed back, and she tried to speak. But one of the men grabbed her and shoved her into the cabin.

A man thrust the torch into my hand. The green light flickered against the faces around me, the desperate pain marking the Torch Keeper's forehead. I stepped forward.

Fire met thatch.

In an instant, the roof exploded with light. Sweet smoke filled my lungs, but I pulled away. Turning my back to the city, I set the torch in its place at the gates once again.

Screams exploded in the air—fire crackling, a baby crying. The door of the cabin lurched, but our men had ensured it couldn't open. Parts of the roof began to collapse in smoking heaps, falling onto the little, glass window, shattering. Broken fragments littered the ground by my feet.

I waited by the gates, ready to race back to our camp. Yet the smoke followed me. Clung to my clothes. I breathed it all in, and somehow I liked it.

Adrenaline pulsed through my body, my heart thumping with each pulse of blood that burned my veins. In front of the cottage, the Torch Keeper fell from knife blows. The band of raiders followed me away from the city. But one remained.

Ivah thrust her knife in the air. She glanced at me, face wild, blood-red hair sharp around her shoulders. Color burned her cheeks. "I'll kill them all!" She threw back her shoulders and gave a delirious laugh as if nothing could stop her.

At once, men with staffs rushed around her. They burst out of the city to destroy us, but we fled into the desert. As I turned one last time, the green fire towered over the city walls. Several figures lay lifeless in the gate, one with red hair sweeping across the sand. Ivah—dead.

I felt Nura's rock sinking into my pocket, but I ignored it. Hardness marred my forehead. We ran until our pursuers lost us, and then our group slowed to a walk. Our chests heaved, a stitch growing in my side.

And I fingered my knife. Ivah had won. She escaped from this nothingness of killing and death we lived in. After all these years, she was free. It was destiny.

I kept walking. The sky still hung low above me, but the stars hid from sight. It was as if they were afraid to appear before someone who killed a family. They weren't courageous like me. Not a warrior like Rekém said I was. My body ached from healing wounds, but I stood taller, braver.

Or maybe the stars escaped from this violent world like Ivah did.

I rubbed my eyes, swollen from smoke, and inhaled deep. I was strong. This was my calling.

27

Rekém

questions no one can answer

Nine months later…

I surveyed the group before me. The army I came with several months ago had nearly doubled. As we set up tents in a grove of trees near the Sea, I wandered through the encampment. Men saluted me, standing at attention as I walked past. I never nodded, never smiled. Leaders weren't friends, they were in charge.

Salty air cut my face. I inhaled sharply but shoved away the memories. Reaching the corner of the camp, I found my own tent already made. A child bowed before me and scurried away. Here, away from the rest of camp life, I stood and surveyed the free world. Trees hung low with silvery moss like spiderwebs. Desert sand slowly changed to smooth pebbles. And then, the Sea.

Home.

I gritted my teeth. This wasn't home. I had visited my homesite, the place where Papa raised me and Teion, but it was gone. Not even ash remained. How many rains did it take to rinse away the last remnants of life? Why couldn't it wash away my memories too?

Shadows flickered in the twilight. Half a dozen warriors appeared, saluting and standing at attention before me.

"Welcome, men," I said. A wisp of hair brushed my forehead, and I shoved it away. Reaching in my belt, I pulled out a map and adjusted it for them to see. "We've been on this mission for nine months. Now is the time to finish it."

They drew closer as I let my forefinger rest against several spots on the map, along the thick black line where the words "The Sea" swept near.

"Each of you will take a cohort and search through these last six cities. And I will lead the remainder of the army to the seventh city. Together, we'll draw out the faithful and lead them back here," I pointed, "to this camp. And then back to the desert where our Prince will lead us."

I pointed to each man individually, directing him to the city I had chosen. "Perth, the north-most city. Tabgha here. Arbelan and Hipios, Gade and Emmartha all to the south. I'll take this one," I tapped the last city on the coast. "Isin. After that is completed, I have one last mission and will send my men back here to await my return. All clear?"

"Yes sir," they said in unison. Waving them away, I found myself alone in the dusk as I surveyed the map.

Isin. The city by the two rivers. And maybe there I would be able to find what Teion sent me here for—a past I could leave behind forever. But first I needed to find the stories Papa told me. To find his Oasis.

I lay on my bedroll with the tent flap still open. Stars shone, scattered between the branches of the trees. The sticks' stringy silhouettes veiled my vision, but several of the celestial bodies still caught my eyes. They sparkled blue and began to dance in the heavens. Shining like Kadira used to.

I let out my breath. She *used* to. Somehow, Kadira had changed. Her grey eyes and deadly passion weren't the beauty I once knew her as. But one day I'd escape everything and be free from this blood and death. I'd hide here by the Sea forever. Alone.

As I fell asleep, I wondered if I could ride on a flame-wing into those stars, to a place where I could finally live free and leave the wars and confusion behind.

Isin's gates spread wide before my army. On my left and right, two separate rivers flowed parallel toward the great Sea far beyond us. And upstream, where the riverheads met, I would find what I was looking for. But first, the cohort of men behind me had a mission to complete.

At the city gates, a young woman came out to greet us. I caught my breath at her porcelain skin and gold-spun hair, hanging down in curls around her shoulders. Her eyes smiled with a laughter all their own as she curtsied before me and beckoned us toward the city.

"Welcome, my Lord." She held out her hand, and I kissed it. Her face curved upwards in an airy smile. "Isin, the city of the

Prince, has not seen such a great army for many ages, and we will set up a feast to welcome you warmly. Is there anything I can supply to bring you comfort, my Lord?"

"Ah, is Isin a city of the Prince?" I asked. "Do I come finding many loyal souls?"

"Very many," she said with a laugh.

I smiled. "I am greatly pleased. We came to seek out your loyalty, and it is refreshing to discover many willing people already waiting for the Prince's command."

The girl pressed her dyed lips together in a smile. My gaze swept across the emerald tunic draped gently around her shoulders and hanging down nearly to her waist. Leggings revealed slender legs and feet with painted toenails.

My cheeks warmed, but I lowered my voice. "Perhaps a word with you? May I send my men into the city while we converse?"

"Of course." She stepped to my side as my men entered Isin. When the last man left us, her chin turned up toward mine, cheeks raised, soft. "My Lord?"

Her fingers slipped around my arm. They were warm. I nearly pulled myself away, thinking of Kadira. But the thought faded, and I let myself look down on the beauty before me. Somehow, her dark eyes sparkled.

"My men have come to gather the faithful. We have an army, and we welcome new recruits to join our forces as we prepare to conquer the rest of the kingdom and establish the Prince as the high ruler." I stopped and let out my breath. "But I have come here for another reason."

She waited, watching my face.

"I need to find the Oasis."

The girl inhaled sharply. Her smile returned quickly, but something clouded over her forehead. "My Lord, it has been guarded these many years. None may enter it." She turned her eyes to the ground. "The King banished us from that paradise long ago."

"Nevertheless, I will seek it," I declared. My voice lowered. "Can you direct me to it? And while I am gone, will you show hospitality to my men until I return?"

"If it pleases you, my Lord." She swept her hands toward the rivers. "One must follow both rivers to their roots. There, they are said to join two other rivers. Where they converge, the Oasis is found. Yet none have been able to pass within, my Lord."

My jaw tightened. "None yet." I stopped, glancing up, and my heart beat faster. "May I ask for your name?"

"Of course, my Lord," she said, blushing. "I am Alee."

Alee. I whispered. Brushing back the stray curls on my forehead, I bowed low. "Then I thank you, Alee, most graciously."

"I hope you find the answers you seek." Her voice called out to me, soft. "And I shall look forward to your return."

At the edge of the rivers, I swung back to her. Her cheeks, pale pink, made my throat dry. I nodded to the damsel. "And I you."

My eyes set on the horizon. The rivers wound through the land, and my legs hurried forward to discover the treasure—to discover the past, so I could finally let it go.

28

Rekém

wistful Oasis never dreaming
that eternity rises

Adrenaline rushed through my body. I heard it once said that excitement erases hunger, but it wasn't true. The sun set and rose again above me, and my stomach twisted like angry storm clouds. My shadow shrank until the noon sun erased its marks. Still I pressed forward.

Wind snagged my hair as if trying to steal the gold circlet I wore. I pulled my shoulders back, fighting the air that slipped off the river. My muscles began to tremble with every swing of my arms as the sun beat down on me.

A wild sabbax deer looked at me as I passed. His antlered head lowered to graze on the river rushes, but I trailed away. Water splashed in crystal droplets as the river danced. A bird flew down in an arch and up again. Down then up. Across the river, his song filled the air as if the river itself was the melody and he was the singer.

Who was I? The intruder of their music?

I slipped off my shoes and let my hardened feet slip into the river's frigid water. The calluses on my heel burned for a second. Then they froze, embraced the cold. Tingling swept across my toes, and then they became numb.

I took the first step, creating a wave with my foot and sending new cold chills spiking up my legs. Smooth pebbles shimmered as I advanced upstream.

My reflection watched me. The water ripples broke it to pieces, but I could still see my face. The lines that cut deep. The tunic that hung on my arched shoulders, revealing my collarbone. I rubbed it and tried to massage the tight muscles behind my neck.

A twig snapped somewhere, and my chin jerked. The trees grew closer together here. Evergreens with tightly-knit needles and soft, golden beds underneath. Spiderwebs crossed among the boughs and watched me. I slipped nearer, smelling the fresh scent of wood, deep green needles, and moist ground. The branches were thick by the base and climbed, twisting upward to tiny fingers of twigs clasping onto the needles. Small among the big. Me. Here.

But no. As I curved around a bend in the river, it shriveled away. The sides closed in to create the riverhead, creeks flowing into a larger being. And then between the trees on my right, I caught a glimmer of blue-green. Another river. The place where the four riverheads converge. Wasn't that what Papa told me so long ago?

I stepped out of the river. Water fell in rivulets down my legs, around the curled, black hair and scars. I felt myself drawn forward to the place where the riverhead began. But as the waters grew narrow, trees thickened. They tried to cut me as I pushed them aside with my hands. A cone fell, smacking me on the shoulder. But I pressed through. Ignored the scratches. Spider webs in my face. Slippery, wet needles underfoot. The rhythmic brushing of my body against branches and my feet in muddy ground.

A creature scurried away. Then I stepped into a clearing.

And stopped. Stared. Fell to my knees.

The riverheads drew closer and closer together, the one on my left and the other on my right. But they never met. Where their waters began to near, to almost flow together, the trees halted. Ground stopped. In a world of perfect silence and clear, aqua air, time itself paused.

Before me towered a wall of fire, burning straight to the heavens. The flames burned my eyes in crystal whiteness. They shone like the river—flowing, growing, and dancing to a song only it heard. But it was more. The fire never paused, never halted. It burned tall yet with total, complete silence. No birds called. Even the waters themselves halted their voices.

No heat seared me as I knew it should. A cool, misty breeze rushed in from across the rivers and swept over my body like the feeling one got when standing at the edge of a waterfall where drops shower down in gentle spray. Yet the booming of the waterfall was replaced by a stronger, somehow louder, silence.

My knees buried in the ground as I knelt before the flaming tower that separated me from the paradise the King had created. This fire that banished my ancestors from the Oasis when they made a simple mistake.

But I knelt mostly because of the Presence that fell upon me like heavy dew. There was something deeper, a treasure I could feel with the air that brushed the wall of fire. It was a faint scent on the wind, like when I used to run home from the Sea to smell my papa cooking sweet pastries over the fire, just for me. But now, my mouth didn't water. My whole body did. It tightened, squeezed, burned.

Here was something I had searched for so long. In the stillness of this quiet place, there was peace. Harmony.

Peace that ruffled the leaves and needles of the trees. Peace that made the flowers grow. Peace that gave the riverheads their coolness, the sky its intense yet gentle blue color, and my body a strange yet calming quietness.

Peace.

Maybe that was what was wrong. Living in Érkeos, we twisted what was beautiful in the Oasis and turned it to an ugly mess. Our lives were broken, shattered. But we only pressed forward for more, worked for more, when what we really needed was right here: to be still and know. To know, to find this lost harmony.

But how did one find what we lost? How could we fix what was broken when the fiery wall separated us from paradise?

Or maybe that was the King's point. Perhaps he banished us from peace to watch us stumble and fall as we tried to find it again. Life was a cruel joke.

If only one could find peace, even in the pain of this world. I just didn't know how. Did anyone?

My fists clenched. I grabbed a pebble and threw it hard at the fire. It melted immediately in the glowing heat as if it never existed. My chest tightened as I grabbed another fistful of rocks and slugged them forward. The peace broke. If I tried to steal into the Oasis, I would be just like those stones.

"Why?" I screamed. "Why would you destroy the Oasis we used to thrive in? Why would you banish your people to live in the burning desert? Your people claim you are love. What love is that?" My voice lowered, and I let my chin fall. Every breath shook my chest. I raised my palms to my face and closed my eyes hard. "Why would you let my papa be taken away and leave me to live a life I never wanted to have?"

My voice cut the silence, but that stillness swept around me again. As I lifted one leg to raise myself off the ground, I caught a slip of color out of the corner of my eye.

By the edge of the nearest river, a handful of flowers bloomed, shining from the continual mist dancing down. Their petals rose together to form a curving crescent, just a slip of color. But their faces stained deep red, like blood.

I reached for a blossom to pull it between my rough fingers but stopped. The thin stalk quivered in my hands. When I let my arm fall, the flower bent to kiss the soil, crimson against deep brown.

"The moon-flowers." I breathed. "Just like Papa said."

The crescent petals clasped tight in their scarlet hold and kissed the dirt as if they truly had been formed by the dust of the moon. When the stars first shone and the moon was high, did these flowers see it all? Did they watch the moon fade in the horizon when it sank for the last time? Did they see my ancestors as they were banished, the wall of fire shattering their home, hiding it forever?

I wondered if the moon-flowers saw the King. Why would he plant such beauty and hide it here for no eyes to find?

But I found them. Did the King put them here for me?

I fumbled to push up the wilted flower, but it sagged lower to the ground as if my touch itself was toxic to its broken sides. Like the way I broke Kadira when I seared her shoulder.

I backed up slowly, but my eyes couldn't leave the silent fire and the wilting moon-flowers. Beyond the wall waited an Oasis, a perfect haven of peace and beauty. Only steps away. And yet an eternity I could never grasp nor hope to reach.

I hesitated at the edge of the trees. Perfectly round, yellow berries hung in the fingers of a tree like a splatter of paint escaping from its canvas. I raised my hands to touch them but then stopped.

Who was I to intrude into a world locked away in secrecy for so many years? Nothing changed in the scene before me. I wondered what it felt like when my papa stood here, those years ago when he left everything to follow his King. The same separating fire. The same lostness. The same magical flowers growing, waiting for the moon to rise again. The King who stole everything from us.

If only I could find what was lost, fix what was broken. If only I could find the peace that the flames burned to ashes. But how could I?

"You could." I spat at the fire the King had sparked. My jaw tightened. The King could fix what he destroyed, but he didn't. That was why I would fight until I destroyed him.

As the last month of our mission closed, I stood tall before my army of men. New faces mixed among the old. Knives rose; cheers were raised as we prepared to set out, away from the Sea and back toward our army base in the desert land.

I curled my hands into fists. But I didn't feel anything. The sea behind us shimmered like a thousand diamonds, yet it only reminded me of the wall of fire that blocked me from the place that used to be home. The silent burning mirrored the emptiness in life, the walls keeping me from being who I was meant to be.

An army followed me. They thought I was brave and wise, strong and courageous. But I stared at the desert and wished it could fade back into the gentle riverside, the trees glowing in hues of green. Not the sharp cacti, hidden scorpions, and burning secrets.

Why did the past have to die?

A hand squeezed mine. I looked down towards Alee, her cheeks pink and raised towards mine. Her hair was pulled up in a loose bun, and gold curls hung around her face.

"My Lord, it's okay to seek answers, to be confused." Her voice caressed my ears. "Commanders don't have to be perfect."

Something grew tight in my chest.

"Leave the past behind. There's always time for new beginnings." Her fingers crawled up my arm, and goosebumps followed.

My throat tightened. "If that's true, why didn't the King offer a new beginning? Forgiveness?"

She didn't answer for a few seconds. Her hand dropped to trace the pattern of the knife in her belt for a moment. Finally, she raised her head, confusion lining her forehead. "Maybe the King is waiting for the perfect time, his future kingdom. But he's too late. Our Prince will conquer all, and he will bring us a hope and a future. Isn't that what we're fighting for, my Lord?"

I nodded, but somehow the answer didn't satisfy. Did the King have plans bigger than we ever imagined? His kingdom was slipping into our hands. But would a King give up his people that easily? What if it was all a trap?

I shook my head. As I walked beside Alee, the army drew around us. We marched forward for liberation. We could change Érkeos forever. We could bring salvation.

She glanced at me. The softness of her brown eyes melted mine. It made my heart beat faster. We were together. The same. Not the separating, too-pure past and blue eyes of Kadira who had turned into a monster. Somehow, this woman was the same as me. We were a team.

Nothing could stop determination. Nothing except maybe love. And the King's false love was what fueled us forward to burn even brighter against him.

Alee and I pressed on together for the Prince's cause. To bring purpose to life.

29

kaдira

now an enemy,
fighting for something she can't see

Another mission. I took a deep breath and heaved an empty bucket onto my shoulder at a city's gates. Hard splinters pierced my cheek. I pulled a thin veil around my face, watching the world through the mask.

We'd already been on so many missions to spy out desert cities, but this was a new city, another mission. Chills snuck up my arm like the flame-wings as they soared straight into the midnight skies. We were the Liberation. Every city mattered.

I eyed a passing wagon with a bundle of hay, pulled by two sabbax deer. The driver of the wagon twisted to meet my gaze. He nodded and propelled the animal forward. A tunic covered the man's belt, but the outline of a knife was barely visible under it.

Behind me, I remembered the handful of other warriors, all concealed under peasant's garb. My own knife hid safely as I paused by the city gate and rested my bucket on the hard ground. Our mission: find the city's weakness.

The writing above the gate curled in letters I struggled to decipher. For a moment I wondered—wondered if this city could be the one from my childhood long ago. All those passing years blurred my memory, but I slowly made out the name—Outha: *City of Wealth.*

Ah, a rich city. A smile touched my cheek, although I felt something sink deep inside. It wasn't home. Mama and Daddy's city had a different name. I'd forgotten it, but if I ever found it again, I'd know it, somehow.

I eyed the torch that burned an unusual shade of blue-green. With just the slightest touch, the city would turn to our side, become liberated by our fire. This was our mission, and I pushed away the my memories.

As the crowds disappeared into the city, I stepped towards the torch. My hand slipped into my pocket. Then, raising my hand, I let flecks of black powder stain the fire. Blue vanished to green.

I spun around and entered the city. Streets spread around me, lined in lush flora. Sprinklers sprayed waterdrops, and my feet met well-paved streets of grey granite. As I walked along, windows peeked at me with ivy tickling their clear panes.

I moved the bucket to my other shoulder as the city square opened before me in soft hues. No cactus grew on the streets, but a lean tree quivered in one corner. Booths of violet tapestries and silky tassels lined the street as businessmen called out their wares. I shot them a small smile and passed by with a flicker of my lashes.

Away from the booths, a well bubbled up into a fountain. Women leaned their buckets into the cool spray and chatted as they let the water give them a break from the desert sun. I melted into the crowd, pretending to wait for my own turn.

One woman with a tight, yellow shawl ducked her head as a taller lady drew near. The second woman had full lips and darkly lined eyes, her forehead smooth and almost pale. She raised her chin to the first woman and let her voice grow in intensity. I slipped closer to listen.

"You foreigners think you know everything!" The tall woman declared. She shoved her bucket into the water and placed one hand on her curved hip. "Go ahead then. Follow your King or your Prince, and see if they do any good! But don't try to force religion on us, you low-living peasant." She swung the bucket onto her arm and turned to leave.

The woman in yellow spoke softly. "You can't live undecided. One cannot serve wealth and prosperity alone."

"I've been doing it for three decades, and see what it's brought me?" The tall woman motioned toward the fountains and the richly clad merchants. With her sharp fingernail, she tapped on the granite stone. "This is my King."

"Ah," the woman said, "then you have already chosen. One who serves wealth is one who follows the Prince and his ways."

"I serve no one!" she yelled after her retreating comrade. The taller woman swung around and nearly toppled against me. I stumbled out of her way but froze when I saw her eyes. They shone cloudy blue-green. *A Torch Keeper.*

The woman averted her gaze, but mine followed her. Her velvet dress disappeared into the crowd of sellers. Another sharp elbow found my side as someone behind me urged me to quicken my pace.

I slipped between women to fill my bucket. Their voices rose as they chatted about the jewelry that ran in their families, and I tried to nod at their references to "sardius" and "topaz" gems. Yet my mind raced elsewhere.

As I left the city, I tarried by the gates. Sunlight poured in from the desert, and I wiped sweat off my forehead. My shoulder ached from the heavy bucket. In the sand, mirages of water mixed with dust clouds from the soles of weary travelers. But behind the city, the gentle fragrance of water and flowers kissed the air.

Another woman joined my side, and I nodded to her. She touched the knife under her dress, staring into the wilderness.

"Any findings?" she asked.

I nodded. Glancing around, my own voice cracked in a whisper. "The city has already chosen our cause. We don't even need to fight."

She raised an eyebrow. "Liberation." Her hand touched her shoulder where her scar matched mine.

When our comrades joined us, we escaped from the city. I turned back briefly and eyed the green fire that welcomed travelers. A figure reached for the torch, then stopped. The Torch Keeper looked at the emerald flames and shrugged. Her eyes met mine before she spun away.

The woman I had encountered earlier at the well entered the Torch Keeper's dwelling, and my cheeks rose with a smile. A battle wouldn't even be necessary. The city was already ours.

We twisted through the familiar haunts behind the dunes and sweeping sandbanks. At the head of our encampment, our group stood by Teion's dwelling and nodded as he opened the door.

"Ah, good news I hope, my spies?" he asked.

Another warrior stepped forward. "The city's already taken. Even now, the people are eager to embrace the Prince and be liberated from their former ways of thinking."

Teion nodded with a slight smile. "Like the last towns we've turned. Perhaps the tides are finally changing for good." He marked out something on his map and clasped his hands together. "We will stick with the easier methods then. Select a score of our best thinkers to move into the city to turn their minds, and they'll surrender to our cause without a battle. We will keep the city as a base until further needed." His voice lowered. "Well done. Soon the kingdom will thank you for your valiant deeds."

The group nodded, and we turned to leave. Teion stopped me.

"My dear." He motioned for me to step in the room as the others left. Shivers ran down my arms as he strode over to a cushioned chair in the corner and sat down to relax.

I nodded.

"You have done so well—very surprising indeed." His eyes met mine. "A valuable part of our entourage, I'm sure. And you've been here but a few years?"

"Five." I bowed my head. "I thank you, sir."

"Only five years," he murmured to himself. Nodding, Teion traced a line on the map, and paused on a squiggled line. He drew a circle around it with his fingernail and looked back at me. "Soon, I will entrust you with more. Are you prepared for that?"

Heat rushed to my face. "I would be honored."

"Good." Teion waved his hand toward me. "You may be going now, my dear. But be prepared. I have a mission for you."

When I exited the room, a blast of hot air made me blink. I let it blow against my hair as I slipped around a crowd of marching children. Someone sharpened knives, making a high-pitched ringing, and the smell of roasting venison rose around me.

Behind a row of buildings, I caught a glimpse of one of my comrades as he began to train a group of new teenagers. Their arms swung with glimmers of silver on their knives. Every thrust had to be done perfectly. I eyed one boy in the corner who stumbled through the practice, watching the girl beside him for directions.

I shook my head, joining in the crowd of onlookers. Several pointed at the boy and laughed, and the trainer's eyes turned sharp on his stumbling movements. The man stalked towards the boy.

But before the fun could began, I caught a glimpse of black in my peripheral vision. My head snapped to the side, and something in my chest fluttered.

I rushed toward the retreating figure as he slipped between two buildings. My feet stumbled, but I caught myself, raising a hand to my throat and forcing my lungs to take a deep breath.

Color burned my cheeks as I ran past a tent and let my eyes sweep across the man standing before me. "Rekém, you have retur—?"

The words caught on my tongue. My body grew cold. I stared at Rekém's dark hair slicked back from his forehead, the circlet caressing it, the eyes that stared so deeply into mine.

He twisted toward me with the same lazy grin, but his hands clasped tightly around another woman's waist. She stared at me with a glimmer in her eyes, perfect cheeks touched with pink, and gold-spun hair curling lightly around her face.

"Who is this, my love?" she said with a slight laugh that made Rekém turn his back to me.

"No one in particular." Rekém leaned toward her.

The world began to spin around me, and I fled.

30

Rekém

he climbed up
but only slipped further down

Teion paced behind the table lined with battle plans, maps, and candles flickering shadows onto the walls. His eyes scanned me with tight lines creasing their sides. "Rekém, I'm ashamed of you."

"The feeling is mutual." I offered a gracious smile.

"You brought me five hundred warriors and a woman who stole your heart." Teion snorted and turned his back to me. His arms crossed, making a dark silhouette against the flickering candles like the night closing around the rippling Sea. "When are you going to *grow up?*"

I grabbed his shoulder and swung him around to face me. My fists curled like talons as I spat in his face. "I've done everything you asked. When will it be enough?"

He raised an eyebrow. "Why, that's a question. You want the answer, the *real* answer, Rekém?" His fingers dug into the neck of my cloak and jerked me forward. Cut off my breath. Teion's words pierced me like a knife. "Nothing. Nothing is enough." His fists twisted, and stars blurred my vision as he pulled close. His hot breath burned my face. "I'm the leader here; stop trying to steal my honor. You're always going to be a failure, little brother."

When he released me, I pulled at the neckline of my tunic, gasping. My heart pounded. Teion stepped back and held up his nails to the candlelight. He tore off a piece of one nail and threw it on the ground.

"You know, I've always been a very busy individual," he said.

I waited, watching the smirk grow on his face. My chest heaved for breath.

"Every time you mess up, I judge you. So I'm really pretty busy, because I'm judging you, let's see…" Teion counted on his fingers and smiled. "All the time."

I winced. When I tried to inhale, my lungs shook, and I pressed a fist against my chest. I let my vision drop to the ground.

"Teion, I never wanted to steal your fame," my voice broke. "I just wanted to be like you."

He laughed, mocking. "You can keep trying forever, but you'll never be like me. You can't be as brave, as strong, as I am. I'm a Prince, and who are you? You've always been too weak, like your father was. He's dead now. Dead! And you're going to be just like him, believing in those silly stories, living in the past. The Oasis can't save you from who you are—a failure."

I clenched the dagger in my belt. We stared at each other like two warriors in a duel. The same anger flashing from our eyes. The same locks of black hair falling onto our foreheads.

My hand dropped.

Teion laughed. He sauntered to the corner of his tent and plucked a crimson fruit. His knife slivered off pieces that he slipped into his mouth, juice dripping down the corners of his lips. The slurping sound of his tongue against smooth lips made my stomach flip.

"You're so indecisive." He held his knife against the light and squinted. "You never gave up the past, never moved on. And now you've got a brand-new girl and broken the heart of one of my favorite warriors. What's Kadira going to do without you?" His mouth turned upward, sharp.

"That's not my problem."

"No?" Teion leaned forward on both elbows. "But if it changes who she is, it will be your problem. We can't afford for her to return to the King."

I dug at the ground with my foot, my chest tightening.

"With the new men brought from the Sea," Teion left out my name, "your *Prince* has commissioned you to begin the mountain raid we've waited for so long. Kadira's home, I hear. It's her turn to face her past. Let's hope she's stronger than you. More faithful?"

I slammed my fist onto the table in the middle of the room. "And when have you been faithful to someone other than yourself? Or could no one ever love you because of the person you've become? You're a tyrant, Teion!"

His forehead creased, but he quickly replaced it with his usual smirk. "A tyrant? Strong language there, little brother." He shifted, and his feet scraped against the ground. "Perhaps I'm too strong to need someone else in my life. It would only hinder my enormous potential."

I spat on the ground by his feet.

He clapped his hands together and laughed. It reminded me of a mockingbird's raspy cry. Teion slivered off another corner of his fruit and offered it to me. I shook my head.

"Be that way," he said, "but despite your many weaknesses, I have great plans for you, little brother."

"What if I'm not interested?"

"You are."

I shook off dust from the edge of my tunic. My eyes never left his, watching like an eagle on guard against predators. Teion cut off another piece of fruit and slipped it into his mouth.

"After we destroy the mountain pass, they'll need a new leader. I'd be glad to get you out of my sight, and you'd be out of the desert you hate so much." He leaned forward. "Ruling over a key city, Rekém. What say you?"

I thought back to my time in Palatiel, the lush trees and cool, mountain air. It wasn't the Sea, but the rock and sand-free land offered endless possibilities. One city could grow into so much more.

"I'll consider it." I mumbled the words, and Teion's eyebrows raised.

"Consider it? You're already signed up," he laughed.

I recoiled. "Who signed me up?"

"I did." He shuffled the maps and documents on the table before finding the one he wanted. Little "v" shapes lined one side of the paper as the mountains swept away on the western edge of Érkeos. The city that would be mine marred the entrance to the ridges. "I'll remain in this encampment and send you off. I prefer not getting my hands dirty. Also, I must be here in a fortnight for a critical council with our generals. What a pity if no one could hear the Prince's immense wisdom."

I clenched my fists together. How did one serve the Liberation his whole life and never get the honor he lived for? What reward did I get?

When I ran my fingers through my hair, they snagged on the golden circlet, but I ignored the moisture that leapt to my eyes. My head tossed back. Was that sliver of a crown my only honor for a lifetime of service to the Prince?

"I see your impatience. Characteristic of you, is it not?" Teion drew a pen forward and circled the mountain pass on his map. "Focus, little brother. Your army will camp here." He pointed at an area on the far western end of the desert. "I simply want you to overcome the leaders of the city. The civilians will turn easily, making your conquest a simple one. You may remain in Palatiel until we choose to liberate the rest of the mountains. We'll join you shortly, I'm sure. In the meantime, you can be the constable or general or whatever you desire."

"And Kadira?"

"She's yours," Teion said. "Do whatever you want with her and your other woman. But if Kadira shows any sign of turning," his voice lowered, steady, "then she must be destroyed. Traitors are dangerous."

A call outside the tent made me jerk and pull to the side. Teion nodded, and the corner of his lips turned up. "The rest of our warriors are here. Grant them entrance, won't you?"

I stepped to the door, but Teion stopped me with a raised hand. The candles reflected, their green flames in his glittering eyes.

"Rekém, you must not fail me."

kaδira

parched ground giving up,
letting go

I stepped inside the tent with the other warriors. Teion and Rekém stood before us like twins, lazy smirks on both faces and sharp black hair that touched their brows. I avoided their gaze and stared down at the map on the table.

"This mission is top priority." Teion cracked his knuckles and pulled a knife from his belt. He used it to trace the mountain line on the western side of the map. "Our spies came back with conflicting reports. But one thing is clear—we must take down the gateway before we can storm the mountains."

My eyes traced the creasing lines that spread across the parchment. Triangles formed pointed mountains that cut around the desert like a tiara on the head of a princess, except this tiara slipped, only touching the left side of the map. Within the rocky crevices, markings representing towns faded away to blank paper, marked by a scattering of volcanoes. The unknown world stared us in the face. Only one city stood out on the map, circled with dark ink: *Palatiel*.

Teion bruised the word with his fist. "We must investigate and then destroy the beliefs of these people. They hold the key to the mountain pass, to the faithfulness of the highlanders. If we place doubts in their minds, everything else will fall."

My breath inhaled sharply. I forced my words to keep from cracking. "So we're not destroying the city, only turning it to our side."

"Exactly." He twirled a quill pen in his fingers, the feather combing the air. "But every mouth that does not shut must be silenced."

My lips twisted, and I cocked my head. Teion ignored me and nodded to the rest of the group. Strong men and women towered by my side, each with the same passion burning in their eyes.

"This raid belongs to Rekém." Teion raised an eyebrow at Rekém from across the table. The wrinkles around his lips rose slightly. "If it fails—it's on his shoulders. If he wins," he shrugged, "make the Liberation proud."

Rekém lowered his chin with a nod.

"And Kadira." Teion's voice held a hint of humor. "This is your hometown, I hear. You will be beside Rekém in everything. This is your chance to take revenge on those who deserve punishment, but you're also our source of inside information. Make this beautiful." He stood and swept his hand around the room, meeting each warrior's gaze. "You will embark in half a fortnight's time. May your *Prince* be glorified."

As we exited the room, I reached for my knife. I tried to crush it in my fist, hoping the hilt would shatter into a million pieces and litter the ground. My heart pounded like a hammer on an anvil as fire billowed around it. How could I go back? How could I face a past I had thrust away?

Rekém crossed in front of me, headed to the opposite end of camp. I grabbed at his tunic and jerked him toward me. He turned and let his gaze wash over me. Our eyes locked. A sweep of black hair caressed his forehead, and I almost brushed it aside—almost reached to touch him as if everything was like it used it be.

"You need to explain. Right now," I hissed through my teeth.

He offered a crooked grin and pushed his hair away from his eyes. "Explain what?"

A glimmer of the stars shone in his pupils. My shoulders dropped, and I turned half away. "I don't understand," I said, my lips cracking. "I thought you cared. I thought you loved me. What happened?"

His face tilted, masked in the shadows. "I did love you, Kadira. One time. I loved the beautiful person you were."

"I'm still me." I grabbed him again, let my nails dig into his skin. "Nothing's changed."

"No, everything changed. Don't you see? Open your eyes, Kadira, and look at yourself. You're not the woman I loved. You've become like the rest of them—just fighting and killing and thinking you're important. What happened to you?"

When I couldn't respond, he continued.

"I can't be tied down. Sometimes love fades; it doesn't always last. And we have to move on, okay? I found someone else."

I pulled away as the words hit me like a blow from a staff. Taking a shaky breath that rocked my chest, I let myself meet his eyes. "How could you just find someone else? I left everything for you."

"No," Rekém laughed mocking, taunting. "No, you left for yourself. You wanted power, and you got that. You wanted revenge, a purpose. Isn't that enough for you?"

Tears burned like fire, but I could only shake my head.

He kicked dust at my feet and turned away. "Go fight a few more battles, become more like the others. You can never go back. You can't ever change. Just forget it all. What's one life anyway?"

Darkness surrounded me like the lies I had grasped onto for so long. They slipped through my fingers, the cold hitting me and stealing my breath away. I tried to pull my dress around my arms, but the sleeveless tunic made my hand meet only air. I touched the smooth scar on my shoulder—the scar he gave me—, and shivering convulsed my body.

I only wanted him. I only wanted someone who would never leave me, someone who understood. But the scar laughed in my face.

He never cared. He just got me into his group and then left me to gasp and sprawl in the sandstorm of lies that stole away my breath. Choked my throat. Burned my vision.

I wasn't enough for him. Or Mama. Or anyone. That's why they all left me.

The scar seemed to burn. I recoiled, but the memories came thrusting through my chest. Rekém grabbing me. The pain. The fire. The aching skin that would never heal.

I stumbled away, falling over a barrel. Catching onto its harsh sides, my palms stung, but I forced myself to stand. My legs tottered. With the barrel at my shoulder height, I leaned against it.

My reflection gazed back at me from the surface of the water in the barrel. The barrel quivered, then become still. I stared at myself, the person I had become. A tall torch nearby cast light in the darkness, green colors.

My wavy hair twisted like claws and was jerked back from a forehead marred by lines. Cheeks dark from the sun were sunken and pulled downward as if locked in a grimace. But I saw my eyes.

Those eyes, the blueness like Daddy's. The glowing sapphire that cried when Mama left me. The irises that hid for so long and finally became unashamed and bold, beautiful because I threw aside the mask, became the person I was meant to be.

But there in my reflection, the eyes staring back at me were dull. Their blueness faded to burnished grey, almost brown like everyone else's. The sapphire color had vanished. It slipped into the desert, burned, marred, and ugly like the façade I hid behind.

I kicked the barrel, but the water remained still. My aching foot throbbed as I hobbled and grasped for my sandals. I reached out, threw sand in the water, tried to erase the image of who I was.

The ugliness remained the same, only now it was broken by ripples, intensifying the horror of my own face.

And I turned away. I let tears wash my cheeks. Rekém was right. I wasn't who I once was. My lips pressed tight, and I sank down against the barrel. Everything he said was true. I wasn't beautiful.

My dull eyes rose up toward the stars. The same constellations watched me—the Torch outlined in stars that always pointed toward the western sky, the Flame-wing that never let down his wings. They were all the same.

But as I followed the Torch's fire with my vision, I could almost see the towering mountains. Palatiel, the mountain pass that soon would fall. And it would be my fault.

I sank against the barrel and let tears wash the dirt off my cheeks.

32

KADIRA

secrets can arouse ransom's letters,
erasing what is past

A quilt of dry land swept before us. Rocks hid under the sand, waiting for the soles of our feet. They waited to cut us open and let blood spill. The sun already beat upon my back. My shoulder blades pulled together, a line of sweat streaking down my spine.

I pulled a veil close around my face as sand pierced the air. My throat pulled tight, and I doubled over coughing as particles clung to my tongue and mouth. Beside me, someone spat out the grit. I tried to catch my breath.

I clasped my small bundle of supplies—two changes of clothing, my water flask, dry food to eat while riding, and a make -shift tent. When I shifted the pack to my other arm, something fell.

I knelt. My muscles tensed, and I stood quickly. But my eyes dropped back to the sand.

The pink pebble Nura gave me so long ago. Somehow, it stumbled out of my garments as if following me. It watched, unblinking eyes, begging for me to remember. To let myself go back. To relive the past.

"Take this," said a small girl, shoving a rope into my hand. I recognized her. The child's fingers had clasped to mine five years ago when I saved her from a raid. When I fought my first battle. But her eyes never left her feet as she pulled herself to the next warrior beside me, pulling another rope, leading another animal. The same, endless life we lived.

She was just like Nura those years ago. But somehow, a different life had broken this girl.

I turned away. My fingers gripped the harsh twine she'd given me. Tied to the rope, a sabbax deer snorted and shied away in glimmering gold. I tried to jerk it forward, but it tossed its head. Horns cut the air.

The man beside me reached to calm the beast, but the deer struggled to pull away. My comrade murmured, slowly running his hand down the deer's spine. The sabbax grew still, and its large, unblinking eyes watched me. The creature's feet swished on the rocky sand as it smacked its side with its tail, keeping its head raised toward me.

But my gaze fell again, and I let Nura's rock slip into my palm. It massaged my calluses as if holding a warm embrace. Like the hugs Nura used to give me. Why did those memories feel so far away in this wasteland of sand?

I shoved the stone back into my bundle of clothes and turned to fasten the pack onto the sabbax.

The animal jerked. I touched its fur, the hair slipping through my fingers as if I tried to grasp the wind. My breath caught as memories swept through me.

"I can't ride this animal," I said, dropping the rope. It fell onto the sand, but the sabbax didn't move. "I can't."

Rekém's glare cut toward me from his own mount. His eyes narrowed. "You will." He waved an arm in the air. "Men, let us ride for the Prince."

A cheer went up from the mouths of the warriors. They mounted and pressed their heels against the animals' sides. Hooves beat the ground.

But I stood by the deer. My hands tightened to fists. How could I ride into the mountains like last time? How could I do it without Mama—ride to kill instead of to save?

Somehow, I gripped the beast's hair and pulled myself onto its back. My knife pressed against my leg as I set my gaze on the horizon. It spilled before me, marred by the silhouettes of an army riding forward.

The deer lurched. I gasped and scrambled for the rope. We were swept away into the dry land, riding in the wind like sand in the desert's storm.

Air whistled around my ears. My veil fluttered, wrapping around my neck, but I couldn't pull it back up. With every lunge of the sabbax, my knuckles turned white. We raced toward the sunset.

When the sun touched the edge of the mountains before us, I caught a stain of black to my left. It swept, wide, then stopped. I let my eyes roam the desert, but they caught on a pile of rubble and smoky ash. An archway leaned at an angle, and wind brushed dust off its trembling frame. A shower of rocks fell.

But I saw more.

Was there once an elegant dancehall in the center of the city? Did children laugh and run out the gates, exploring the desert's unknowns? Did they stare at their own city torch and imagine nothing could ever destroy its light? What happened to those fantasy dreams when the city was brought down to a mound of grime, a memory?

My lips parted in the coolness of the air. The city of the past disappeared behind us, but I wondered if perhaps that was where we lived. Did Mama die there by the city gates as she gave her last breath protecting the torch?

Darkness fell, but we kept riding. Our cavalry strained their necks as they peered into the dusk. One deer stumbled, and a man fell onto the rocky ground. We didn't pause as the army rushed forward, and the man tarried behind us.

Night fell, and day disappeared too. In the dusk on the third day, the desert changed to rocks. Through the shadows, my eyes caught sight of something rising out of the desert. We neared the foot of the mountains. The first tree rose in thick boughs, and Rekém pulled his mount to a flying stop.

"We camp here."

Like a colony of ants working in syncopation, we dismounted and prepared to set up tents. I grabbed my own saddle bags and let them fall. The sabbax deer folded his legs under him, but his chest still heaved with each breath. My own legs quivered as I looked up at the mountains. Only blackness met my eyes.

I knelt to tear apart the bags and make a place to rest. My shoulders fell as I struggled to raise the leather hide and position it standing upwards.

"Not you." Rekém kicked the supplies back down. "We're going up."

I tried to hold back a sigh. My arms ached, but I straightened to meet his gaze. "Your brother said—,"

He cut me off. "I'm in charge here. You're coming with me to the city."

"And if I don't?"

"You will."

Our eyes locked. Mine fell first.

Rekém barked commands to the group and motioned for two other men to join us. We followed the worn mountain trail.

Rocks stuck in my shoes as I struggled to keep up with the men. My legs rushed back and forth twice to match their single, long step. A stitch burned in my side, and I pressed my hand against it.

The path swept up and around until I could see the stark desert behind me. In the dim starlight, it looked like the huge expanse I'd heard about in the stories of the great Sea. If water filled its boundaries, we would be an island standing high above the waves.

But dryness cracked my lips. I followed Rekém toward the flickering blue of Palatiel, the mountain pass.

Lights poured out from the open gates. A torch stood, blue.

My stomach twisted. It wasn't Emyir's torch anymore. A stranger lit the fire because Emyir was dead, and I killed her.

I hurried into the city. Rekém led us through empty streets until we met the city square where music quivered in the air. The dancehall glowed. Shoes tapped in rhythm, and generous laughter mixed with the aromas of soft cakes and pastries that were certain to hold the eye of every young boy.

I almost laughed. Ike would be there. But now he was older, a man. Would I still recognize him?

A couple near the arched doors swayed back and forth to the music. Another man leaned against a wall playing a stringed instrument, and smile wrinkles kissed his face. When he saw us, his face exploded into a grin. "Come join us, weary travelers!"

Rekém's jaw hardened, but he motioned our two comrades forward with a harsh whisper. "Find out any information you can."

They strolled up the marble steps as Rekém's fingers choked my arm like claws and dragged me back into the shadowy streets.

I yanked my arm away. "What?"

His lips twisted to a smile. "Remember what Teion said. Make this beautiful." He snorted. "We must be ready for tomorrow's invasion. Don't let us down. The Liberation is always watching."

And then I was alone.

A sliver of starlight pierced the air. I raised a hand to my face and froze. Calloused fingers looked back at me. Although they were slender like a child's, they had already shed so much blood. My hands clenched into a fist and fell back to my side.

A dog barked, and I jerked away. Footsteps echoed down the street. My eyes darted from one side to the other, and I fled. My feet flew past the garbage-lined alleys. Something fell behind me and rattled as it rolled on the ground. Wind pressed against my face. My shadow flickered against a wall, cut to slices with each row of bricks. I turned another corner and skidded to a stop. Arid sand cut my feet as the dusty road disintegrated into smooth cobblestones that had doubtless been swept by a child's hand.

An archway appeared several stone-throws ahead of me. Coarse, mud bricks lined the front and were edged with shrubs. I froze as I took in the scene before me. Familiar memories began to dance before my mind. My arms hung limp as I was swept away to the past.

There was Mama, holding me. She looked down with a smile, whispering those words I longed to hear again, "Don't forget how much I love you." She touched my smooth cheek. "You are strong, my princess."

But I sank to the ground. Rock and grime scraped my legs as I buried my head in my arms. When I opened my eyes, a blossom rested on the ground. Pink. Mama's favorite color.

I plucked it between my thumb and forefinger. Squeezed. Liquid stained my skin, and the flower crumpled, bled to the ground. Like the moon-flower juice I had poured out so long ago.

My legs grew strong. I started toward the bending flowers that protected the home I had hidden in for so long.

Today was different.

I threw my shoulders back and walked on my own toward the archway. I didn't need anyone now. I was strong. I was brave. Like Mama wanted me to be. She would have been proud.

But my fist hesitated on the door. Memories pierced my mind and stared at me with glittering eyes. The flowers watched me grow up from a trembling toddler to a woman who could stand on her own. I left behind everything I loved so I could be brave like Mama wanted. Now I was powerful, and no one could stop me.

But my chin lowered to my chest. Here, I was only Kadira—the girl who tried to count the stars, dreamed of a friend who would love her, and wanted someone to hold her safe.

The door swung open. A slender woman with strong hands hesitated before me. Her brown eyes paused, and wrinkles turned up in a smile that made a mole quiver on her cheek.

"Kadira, my girl?" She reached for me, trembling, and pulled me into the candlelight. Tears shook on her lashes. "Are you really home?"

Light rushed around me, blue and soft. The same fire flickered under a teapot whose steam blasted the air with sweet smells. Yet the table lay empty. Closed doors hid the children who slept unaware of the death creeping in with the dawn.

My arms pulled around my body. I let my hair fall across my shoulders to hide the ugly scar that stared out so boldly.

From before the fire, a man rose. His eyes softened when they met mine—his pure, dazzling sapphire. A smile crossed Father's jaw as he stepped toward me.

"Oh Kadira!" Gamma choked me in a hug as if I was a little child all over again. She rocked back and forth before pulling away and letting her tear-stained face stare into mine. "You don't know how we missed you. The children will want to know you're here. Nura needs to know. It's been so long…"

I grabbed her arm. "No, Gamma."

"But what about Nura? Kadira, you don't know how this has hurt her." Her voice broke.

I pulled my shoulders close to my body. Looked away.

Gamma swung her arm toward the doorway that used to be my room. "She hasn't spoken a word since you left. She won't smile, won't laugh. Kadira, she needs you."

"Where's Ike?" I laughed bitterly. "Nura never needed me when he was with her."

She raised a hand to her mouth and turned away quickly. Father reached to pull Gamma into his own arms. His gaze pierced through me.

"Ike disappeared after you did," he said. "So did Faine, even though you always fought with him like sand clashing stone. Neither of them ever came back. They needed you." Father shook his head. "Did you know how much you were loved?"

Words clung to my tongue. My eyebrows pulled together, but I shook the thoughts away. "Not Ike. He can't be. Can't be gone." I stumbled backwards. My eyes caught a glimpse of the darkness through the thick curtains, and I straightened. With the burning in my eyes, I could only stumble to a chair. My breaths came in gasps. "But I can't stay. I shouldn't be here."

My elbows fell against the table, and I squeezed my eyes shut. I hid them with my fists, tried to block out the world and the lights that blurred my vision. When I raised my eyes, my chin rested on my hands.

"You must flee. Tonight. We will come at dawn, and if you are not gone..." I looked at my fingers, those blood-filled calluses, and cringed.

"And you are coming with us?" Father slipped his arms around Gamma, but he kept his eyes on me. My own gaze fell.

I shook my head. "This is my war we're fighting. We want liberation. I belong with them, with the Prince."

"We can't leave without you."

I raised my stiff jaw toward Father's face. "You already did. You left me that day in the desert. You turned around and left without saying goodbye." My voice rose to a shrill cry. "Why is this any different?"

Tears lingered in his eyes. "My child," he said, "that was the hardest thing I ever did."

I straightened. "I'm not a child anymore." My voice rose as I stood and stepped back to the door.

"Then why did you warn us?" he asked. "You join their raids. If you are truly a liberator as they are, why did you come back?"

My eyes burned, and I shook my head. "I don't know." So many words mixed in my mind. Ike. Nura. Rekém. My waiting comrades spying out the city. The death that would come.

A knot grew in my throat. I pushed it away and forced my shoulders to straighten. My eyes met theirs, flashing in the dim light. I turned to the doorway without speaking.

"'Dira?" A soft voice begged as another door opened and a figure stepped into the room. Pink edged her cheeks and flowed into round lips. The girl wasn't a child anymore; her toddler hands had disappeared into slender ones, but I could still imagine them, still know how they would feel when pressed against mine. She stumbled toward the table, and sightless eyes searched for me. "Did you come home?"

Nura. I wanted to reach out and hold the blind girl tight as I once had. I wanted to tell her stories and sweep her up in the air. I wanted to embrace her laughter, be her eyes, and protect her from the world as I used to. Nura needed me.

But instead I shook my head and slipped out the door. The midnight shadows embraced me as I fled from the memories. The orphanage wasn't my home anymore. They weren't my family now. They never were.

CRR.

33

KAÐIRA

indecision; if mercy erases limitations,
where is her destiny?

The sky went from midnight to grey and grey to pink as the dawn struggled to life. I sat in my tent, back in the camp of those who fought for our cause. Their snores and heavy breathing lingered in my mind as I tried to claim sleep for myself. We were the Liberation, giving our lives so others could have purpose. Could have a future.

But somehow, liberation didn't seem as beautiful now, when all I could see was the face of my little friend. I pulled my knees to my chin, begging for Nura to be safe. I couldn't protect her anymore. Her pink pebble rubbed between my fingers. She had loved me. She thought I would keep her safe. But I couldn't. And Ike was gone too.

I looked down at the little rock and wished I could throw it as far as the wind could take it. If only I could let go and move on. Forget.

My nails cut into my palms as the shadows began to slither away. Light sliced the air.

A hiss shattered my thoughts, and a woman motioned for me to enter the world outside my tent. I let the pebble fall back into my pocket. Quickly tying a black shawl around my face and hair, I ducked my chin and slipped out of my tent to find the other warriors shoving knives in their belts. Dark garments lined with silver concealed their identities. I met the gaze of a woman with gold-spun hair standing by Rekém's side. Her eyes caught mine. And I hated her. Hated her for how she stole Rekém from me.

Rekém raised his voice in a sharp whisper. "We are not here to destroy the city." He motioned toward the path winding into the mountains. "Palatiel must be weakened. Today we are going to strangle their necks so they'll quickly surrender, turn, and bow the knee to our Prince. If not, we'll leave them gasping until the Prince's armies can attack and utterly destroy the city."

Someone raised a cheer, but he was quickly hushed.

"There are several traitors still faithful to the way of the King. These must be targeted specifically. Kill all resisting adults. Any children we find will be taken captive and trained to serve the Prince. If they resist, we will kill them also," Rekém said, looking at me. "Understood?"

I couldn't nod. Couldn't move.

Rekém separated us into groups. One band would sweep into the city and destroy the Torch Keeper and his family before the city was fully awoke. Other commands rushed around me, but they never met my ears.

Too soon, Rekém turned to me. "Our group's target is in the furthest reaches of the city. We'll break up and meet at our goal.

And, Kadira," his words swung around to slap me, "you'll come with us."

As the sun began to peek above the desert, Rekém led us in silence, his dark eyes trailing the ground. I grew cold.

We were the first ones through the gates. The Torch Keeper had already completed his morning tasks, and he was nowhere to be seen. I thought of Emyir, her body bleeding in the desert sand the night when she had been searching for me. My breath caught in my throat.

An abandoned street turned sharply, and we followed it away from the sunrise. The light created long shadows against the ground, flickering over each loose stone.

The city twisted around us like a snake. I followed Rekém and the other warriors. Icy tendrils began to crawl over my feet, and it sent goosebumps up my legs. My body grew stiff, and my black and silver dress seemed like a weight pulling me down.

We drew near the archway.

And I knew whom they were looking for. Father's eyes were blue. The warriors would murder him and Gamma and every single orphan with them.

"No." A whisper broke my lips. I marched after my fellow warriors, but my feet weren't my own. They stumbled forward without feeling, and my heart begged to leap out of my chest. My eyes rested on some budding flowers, and I looked down to the ground, almost expecting to find a blossom soft from Mama's touch. But it was gone.

Fragrant air swept around us as we crossed beneath the archway. The flowers opened their arms to the world, but no one else seemed to notice. The gate that had welcomed many an orphan now looked down on us, messengers of liberation. And death.

"One," Rekém whispered to the armed group around me as he motioned to the door, "two..."

I never heard his command. The door was thrown aside, and we entered the home with knives in hand. When we found the room empty, my shoulders relaxed. Only Father's bow staff leaned against the wall, but it too was silent. The sole breath of life in the room was the fire, burning blue. I let my lungs exhale.

A side door opened, revealing Father's calm face. His glowing, blue eyes scanned us as he shut the door behind him with a firm push. When he looked at me, he stopped. A black shawl covered my hair and face, but his gaze pierced through my mask. Something like pity seemed to show on his usually serious face. But it was something more.

"Declare your loyalty to the Prince, or we will kill you!" Rekém ordered as he sliced his knife around the room.

Father tore his eyes away from mine. "My children, your Prince has deceived you into believing his lies. He steals your hearts and turns them to stones, cold and without life." His cheeks lifted with a sad smile. "But the King loves you and will give you a heart of flesh that can truly live."

"Will you recant your allegiance to the King and the tyrant government you follow?" Rekém's voice boomed like thunder, a storm ready to destroy everything within its reach. I stared at him, this part of him I had never seen before, never loved.

"Recanting the way of the King is like saying there isn't a sun," Father answered. "Both statements are lies, and I will only speak the truth. The King loves you. He wants you to surrender yourself and come to him."

"Then you all will die, starting with the youngest child within your walls."

The house exploded with action around me. Rekém shoved Father aside, and our warriors tore into the bedrooms. The children would be sleeping there. They couldn't escape. *Nura.*

"No!" I grabbed Rekém and swung him around to face me. "You can't kill children. They are orphans. Helpless! Would you murder them in their own beds?"

His lips curved into a cruel smile. "Of course. Haven't you done the same?" He twisted the knife out of my hand and threw me against the wall. I crashed against the bricks. Pain shot up my arm.

But the memories consumed me. Little children screamed as we killed their parents before their eyes. Houses went up in flames as we fought for our cause. Blood stained the ground, and families were burned alive. It was all in the name of Liberation.

I looked into Rekém's piercing eyes and saw the same darkness there. He turned his knife toward my chest, the blade like an arrow pointing to its target. Rekém laughed, shook his head.

"I knew you were too weak. You failed us." The circlet around his head glistened like a snake. "Traitor."

The world stilled as I stared at the weapon poised to steal my life. Was this what it was like for those I had murdered? One thrust could end a future. Life was a breath of air, gone in a moment.

He pulled back the knife, ready to thrust. Hesitated. I saw conflict in his eyes, the eyes that once burned my heart with passion. They narrowed.

In a millisecond, everything exploded around me. A dark shadow flashed by my arm, and I was thrown aside. Something crashed. Dust filled the air. I covered my head and screamed. Footsteps ran out the door, and the air grew still. Then smoke began to billow.

But death didn't come. I twisted around to stare at the place I had just stood. Blood covered the ground. Deep red flowed free from a stab wound.

The body didn't move.

I knelt down and stared at the one whose life had been traded for mine. Thick eyebrows arched over eyes that would never open again. His red-brown hair, neatly trimmed, was speckled with grey. His face now stilled in death.

"Father?"

Blood poured from the Father who pursued me when I ran from him. Who loved me when I rejected him. Who was a daddy when I had none, taking away my parents' family name and making me his own. His child.

I took his large hand in mine and felt the coarse fingertips. "Please," I begged his eyes to open. "Please be all right. Please come back."

When no answer came, I collapsed. Tears stung my eyes and ran down my cheeks. My shoulders shook. I was again a little child, begging for someone to hold me tight. Someone to protect me—to care.

But he was gone.

34

Rekém

at crossroads, he takes the step, falls,
misses the crown

My knife left my fingers, stained red. I didn't know which body I had stabbed. My lungs exploded, every muscle shoving me out the door. My men followed. Screaming, blood pooling. Someone with a torch threw it onto the thatched roof, and it burst into fire. Our green emblem rose high in the air, like the mountains.

I convulsed. My stomach twisted, and I fled from the house. I left the body of one who would die because of my knife. The other person would burn alive. Either way, Kadira wouldn't escape.

Gasping, my lungs ached. I collapsed against a hard wall. It scratched my back and arms, making dots of blood appear. I lifted my chin raised toward the sky. It was empty.

Wind threw my hair back. It thrust against me with the force of a sandstorm, and I couldn't escape.

I killed her.

Memories of Kadira burned my vision. The first time we met here, the way her eyes made time stop. Kadira and me in the rain, hiding from the world—with us the only two in existence. Sparring together, our bodies pressing tight. Fleeing together from the sandstorms. The way her hand grasped mine for protection. Her upturned lips when I gazed at her.

And I killed her.

No tears came. Only this endless burning in my throat, tightness in my chest. I covered my face with rough fingers to block out the wind, but it still howled in my ears. I wanted to block it out, hide from its shouts.

Teion would be proud of me. But who was I? I wasn't brave enough, strong enough. Could a warrior be scared, broken? Or was I a failure?

Could I ever find the Oasis where I would be really and truly home? Where the moon-flowers bloomed and peace was found? Or would life always be this continual search?

"My Lord," spoke a musical voice by my side. Alee sat down beside me. She touched my arm, leaned her head against me. "This city is now yours."

I reached to wrap my arm around her, and she took my blood-stained fingers in hers. Her eyes met mine.

"The past is behind you, my Lord." She pulled my hands to touch her own cheek. "We will rule this city together. It and I will be yours."

"Palatiel: the mountain pass," I said through broken lips. "Where we leave the past and move on to the new."

I tried to fight the memories still burning my mind, tried to move beyond them. But it was a battle I might never conquer.

She took me to the city square. The dancehall stood tall and glimmering, a thousand colors in the sun. In front of it, citizens murmured together with anxious whispers. Knives and sticks were raised, but the people faced an enemy they didn't understand.

Alee nudged me to climb the stairs to the dancehall. As I stood on the raised platform, all eyes turned toward me. Here I was strong. Here I was in command.

I touched the golden circlet around my hair and raised my chin.

"My people!" I let my voice carry on the wind to the farthest corner of the city. "Today you have been liberated from the chains that have kept you from a greater future. The Prince has rescued you, and I will lead you to become a city that Érkeos looks up to. We will not be merely the mountain pass; we will become everything the mountain contains. We will grow strong, tall; we will tower above all others. And if you follow me, we will reach heights one could have never dreamed. Your children will no longer hunger. Your wives will no longer wish for greater treasures. I offer you everything in exchange for your loyalty. Who is with me?"

There was no moment of silence. The crowd erupted into cheers and chants, rushing around me and raising me up on their shoulders. We marched toward the city gates where the blue torch was taken down and thrown in the dust. Now our emerald fire would burn. We would rise above the desert, a sign to all Érkeos that we were great.

I caught Alee's eye, and she nodded with gentle lines around her full lips. As the people broke into celebration, I turned towards her.

"Shall we rule the mountains?"

Alee raised her curved eyebrows. "We'll make the Prince proud and kill every traitor." She laughed. "Nothing else would be quite so exciting."

35

KADIRA

petitions reaching above unworthiness;
unending salvation

heat seared my face as the house burst into angry, green flames. They climbed high above me. Soon the home would collapse, and I would die. It was what I deserved.

But as I looked down on Father's face, my lips pressed together tight. He died so I could have so much more. *Life.*

"Father," I cried, soft. "I'm sorry. So sorry."

I let his hand slip out of mine. As it fell, I heard a crash behind me.

I jerked to my feet. *The children!* Throwing myself into one of the bedrooms, I scanned the darkness. Empty. I twisted to the next door, but every bed was empty too. Then the third, my bedroom, echoed as I entered. The pictures on the walls curled in the heat, but I ran past them, grabbed a quilt from my bed of so long ago. Leaving the dark room, I hurried to Father's side and draped the quilt over his still body. He deserved more, but that was all I had.

The room grew cloudy with smoke. I coughed and stumbled against the table. Fumbling, I tried to grab Father's staff. The smooth sides brushed my fingers, but a large cut had severed part of the top. I pulled the stick to my chest against my pounding heart, which thumped against the wood like a cry for help.

When I turned, a wall of fire separated me from the door. Emerald flames crept toward me like a stalking beast until they met the blueness of the fireplace. Two colors clashed, rose high, burned bright.

But I leapt through. My hair singed in sickening smells as I escaped the burning house. In the yard, the archway stood empty. Flowers still smiled in the sun. Soon they would die.

I stood there and looked back at the horror. I wanted to reach out, fix the past, and return to be a carefree child again.

"Why?" I asked the crackling air. "Why couldn't I have been the one who died?"

But there was no answer.

Memories began to burn with the growing smoke as if they wished me farewell—Nura standing in the backyard, throwing her first lost tooth. Her words, "I want to always be a happy family."

By my feet, a stain in the dirt. Seeing myself, those years ago, holding the small vial as it bled into the soil. Thinking I was brave.

Those pictures in my bedroom—they would burn to nothingness.

The sky shone with sunlight and mocked the darkness within me. I dragged myself away from the house. It was my childhood haven, now broken. My place of safety had burned in a mountain of flames.

I twisted back toward the house, smoke billowing from it. Even Father's carpentry shop burned with the green fire. There would be nothing left.

Mama told me to be brave. Instead, I had broken everything.

I covered my face and fled. Like a little child, I raced through narrow streets and forgotten alleys. No faces met mine. The roads were abandoned. It was as if Érkeos itself fled from my sight, embarrassed of the monster I had become.

There was only one place I could go. Away from the city, the memories, the torch that burned emerald for the Prince.

But the forest called. Maybe the meadow and stream I had played in as a child still waited. Maybe it wouldn't know what I had done.

Rocky streets bruised my feet as I walked, remembering. When I reached the stretching city wall, I stopped and knelt. Tears cut my eyes. I thrust my hands forward and opened the secret door in the wall. It creaked. I crawled through, but something pricked my mind. Only the Torch Keepers knew about this passage. I was an imposter.

As I left the streets behind and entered the mountain countryside, I followed a nearly forgotten path. Pointed trees grabbed at my dark cloak, but I shoved them aside.

My feet hurried on their own as if remembering the long-ago years I played there as a child. Ike would have grabbed my hand and raced with me through the countryside. We would play happily, far away from the rush of the city. But now he was gone.

And here I was alone, still wanting to be a little child, to escape life and be free.

The forest meadow was the only place where I could be safe. Maybe the wild roses would still be blooming as they did when I took Nura there as a child. But everything was different now.

When the sun beat down on the forest ground, I threw aside my shawl and let my curly hair hang free. The forest felt as empty as I did. All I could see in the ground before me was the lifeblood flowing from Father's chest. The sun's heat seemed to pull energy out of me, and I willed the rays to take all.

Then the trees cleared, revealing the familiar haunts. I froze and backed up a few steps. Behind the wood's haven, Gamma and the children played near a bubbling spring. They didn't know the horror. They didn't see the knives or smell the smoky scent of death. The orphans laughed under the welcome light of a new day. For them, it was nothing more than a picnic morning.

They escaped the city to find peace in the glen. How could I mar that with my blood-stained hands?

I stood there. I wasn't like them, happy and clean. My purpose shattered the moment I trembled before Rekém, watching him thrust the knife toward my chest. If one didn't have something to fight for, what was life?

I turned away. Why had I come? This wasn't my home anymore. The childhood meeting place wasn't mine, not after all I did.

A sob choked in my throat.

"Kadira?" Gamma stood, surrounded by the children, but her eyes found me standing beside the deep forest. She motioned for me to leave the trees and shadows. My fingers brushed against my black and silver dress. Horrors of the past marred the fabric, and my shoulders drooped. The scar on my shoulder burned.

A small child pulled away from the rest. Her blind eyes searched for me. Nura's lips lifted in a smile as she stumbled away from the other children. A red dress swept around her ankles.

I looked at the bow staff in my hands, Father's staff stained with blood. Nura was too pure.

"'Dira?'"

The name cut through me, and I ran. Distance fell away between us as my arms crossed around Nura. Her cheek pressed against mine, and a sweet, flowery fragrance embraced us. She fell, laughing, into my embrace.

"I knew you would come home!" She giggled. "I knew you would come be with me again. I missed you."

I looked at Gamma. Lines creased her forehead, and her lips quivered. She gently took the staff and held it close, offering a smile through her tears.

"He wouldn't leave you behind, Kadira," Gamma said. "Father told us to come here, but he wouldn't leave."

"Why?" I pushed the tears away. My eyes closed tight as pain swept over me anew.

"A true father never leaves his child behind."

Nura took my hands in hers. My blood-stained fingers touched her soft, clean ones. I winced, sinking to the ground. The darkness was too dark, the pain too real.

"Kadira." Gamma knelt to my level, like my own mama had so long ago. "I forgive you. For everything."

My fingers clenched into a fist.

"The King has control, and this is somehow part of his plan."

"But why?" I glanced at the broken staff as a lump grew in my throat. "Why didn't Father save himself and leave me? Why did he let this happen?"

"He loved you," she replied, swallowing hard. "Do you remember when you were in the sandstorm and first found Nura? Even way back then, he loved you. He went into the storm to find you. I told him it was too dangerous, but he looked me in the eye and said nothing could ever keep him from searching for you. Kadira, the world itself can never stand between that type of love."

I turned my face away. Shame poured down through my tears. My shoulders shook as the past engulfed me like a sandstorm, trying to bury me under forsaken dreams.

"I wanted a mission, something to live for." My voice raised, but I couldn't help it. Nura stiffened in my arms. "Why wasn't that enough? Why couldn't I just have my own purpose in life? Mama told me to be brave, but every time I try, everything falls apart."

Gamma's arm brushed my shoulder where my scar still burned. "One doesn't have to fight a battle to be brave, my dear. One has to trust."

"Trust what?"

"That the King has a purpose; that he saved you for a mission only he can accomplish in you. We can't always see his plan, but the King is guiding us in his perfect way to prepare a kingdom of the faithful. And one day he will make everything clear."

I shook my head. "It would have been better if I had never come. If I had stayed Ka-Dara forever, stuck in the little desert town that burned to the ground."

"Oh, my child," Gamma whispered, covering her mouth. "Don't you remember? That's not who you are. Father changed your name for a reason. He knew you—Kadira, his little child— had a purpose so much bigger."

I looked up. "He changed my name on accident. I told him I was 'Ka-Dara,' but he heard me wrong."

"No," she said, "Father loved you. He wanted you to be his own. He wanted you to be free from the past and for the King's good plan."

I gritted my teeth. "He couldn't have a plan for me when I've fought against him for so long."

Gamma smiled, sad. "But, my dear, that's exactly why I can forgive you," she said, "because he does have a plan for you. The King himself offers forgiveness to everyone, no matter how broken. Have you forgotten how loved you are?"

I lifted my head, letting the tears run off my cheeks onto the sand mixed with clay. "I don't understand."

She laughed slightly. "Sometimes I don't either. Maybe that's why grace is so amazing. We don't get what we deserve even when we've broken everything."

When I didn't respond, Gamma took my hand in hers. She pressed Father's broken staff into my fingers and let loose with her own.

"Kadira, you are called to be a Torch Keeper. You can't erase what you've done, but you can start again. Will you stop running and embrace your calling?"

I smiled through my tears. "You sound like Emyir."

"I wouldn't want to sound like anyone else."

The memories rushed back. The sandstorm, Emyir lying there, dead because of me. If I stayed home, she would have been alive. What forgiveness could erase that?

The King can.

The words whispered through my ears like calmness amidst the storm. I let the sun dry the moisture on my cheeks as I choked out the words. "Gamma, I'm so sorry. It's all my fault. The past, everything was because of me." Nura pulled away as I dropped the bow staff and covered my face. "I'm so, so sorry."

Gamma raised my chin, gentle. "Kadira, you're forgiven."

Nura stared in my face. Her blind eyes saw nothing, yet they seemed to see more than I could. Her voice broke through my silent sobs. "'Dira, are you going to stay with us?"

I glanced at the children as they played innocently under the whispering trees. Nura's pale face begged me to be her eyes in the dark world. Gamma nodded, offering me a heart of forgiveness.

"Nura," I whispered, "I always, always wanted a sister."

Her face beamed like the sunshine, and she crawled deeper into my arms. Nura's tiny hands touched my cheeks as she brushed away the tears.

"I missed you."

I let her words soak in as I placed her gently on the ground. A quivering flower stood by my feet, and I plucked it, tucking the blossom behind Nura's ear.

"This flower is pink, my favorite color," I said, feeling Mama's necklace against my throat. Tears fell. "But I love you so much more."

She smiled, big. But as she reached for me, I hesitated and slipped my hand in my pocket. The dried blood on my skin cracked. Peeled.

Nura's rock waited in my palm, warm and clean, as if holding a gentle goodbye to the past.

"I kept this safe for you." I ran my thumb over her white knuckles as I gave her the pebble. "Do you want it?"

She took it, pressed it against her lips. But her hand dropped again, and she put the pebble back into mine. "No. It's yours, 'member? I gave it to you a long time ago." Her eyes lit up in colors she could never see. "But will you lift me up high? I want to feel the sunshine."

I stood and grabbed the bow staff. Sweeping Nura onto my shoulders, her giggles filled my ears, and the edges of her scarlet dress draped around my hair. Father's bow staff stood firm between my stained fingers. A woody smell. Just like when I was a child clinging to Father's chest, begging for someone to keep me safe when everything else fell apart. Maybe that was being brave—letting him become courage for me.

I took the first step. I was a Torch Keeper again, like Mama and Daddy. Maybe one day I could light the flame and set it before a city as a sentinel to all Érkeos, declaring that the land belonged to the way of the King.

I let my feet guide me toward the children. They laughed and ran around me, a swarm of giggling butterflies as we walked away from the past and towards the future the King would guide us to. Together, we began the long journey into the mountains.

epilogue

ceaseless redemption ever altering time in our nation,
scarlet now overtly white

A girl slipped forward into an abandoned glen. Soft sprigs of grass kissed her toes, like a moth's whispering wings as it slips forward in a breath of wind. Dew drops clung in shimmering droplets. Colors glowed in the gentle sunrise—the pale emerald grass adorning sparkling pink blossoms and yellow daisies; the deeper green of the trees surrounded her, protected her like a city wall; and the clear blue reflection of the creek as it paused on its journey, absorbing the crystal sunshine.

She let her legs kneel gentle by the creek-side. Water lapped to touch her skin and pull away, like a child's teasing laughter as he watches bubbles float just out of his reach. The girl paused to take it all in.

The first morning bird called in sweet notes, fluttering above her and then disappearing in the shadows of the trees. The smell of pine mixed with wet moisture on soil, and the water's bubbling showered her in a breathtaking melody.

She reached forward. Her fingers met the clear water, cold against her calluses. But she jerked away. Sweat touched her forehead. Her eyes fell.

When her gaze fell on the water, her hand flew to her shoulder. A scar swept across in ugly shadows, memories that taunted. The brown mark was like the houses she had burned to ashes. The lives she pierced and left bleeding out on the sand. The lies she spread, the hearts she tore.

And it could never leave. One couldn't move on beyond the past.

"But maybe," the girl said softly, as if the words would shatter if spoken too loudly. "Perhaps the past can be ransomed. Forgiven." Her cheeks flushed pink. "Liberated."

Her knuckles cracked with stains from dried blood. Red-brown residue marked her nails. But she plunged them into the water again. Every drop stung from the cold piercing her skin. The water became stained like scarlet. But then, it began to flow clear again. White.

She drew up her hands from the water, and they dripped onto her skirts. The girl pressed the clean, tan skin against her lips. Tears fell.

Taking a shaky breath, she brushed at her eyes. Froze.

There, in the water's reflection, her own face gazed back at her. Those eyes—piercing blue again. Blue like a cloudless, noonday sky, like the King's flame always burning.

Blue like the eyes of a Torch Keeper.

As she raised her gaze to the skies, sunlight peeked through the trees in rays of shining glory. The clouds glowed pink-orange like a baby's skin. They tumbled gently as if reflecting the creek's own face in their own.

She lifted her cheeks to the sunlight and let it wash over her. And there, somehow, it was as if she was finally clean. She couldn't get back those days she lost, the innocence stained by blood. But she could start over. A second chance.

She was still a Torch Keeper.

The characters

Alee (uh-*lee*): "Sublime"
Am-Othniel (Am-*Oth*-nee-l): "Strength of the King"
Emyir (*Ee*-meer): "Watcher of the Fire"
Faine (Fayn): "Seeking Happiness"
Father (*Fah*-ther): "A Beloved Protector"
Gamma (*Ga*-ma): "Grandmother"
Ike (I-ke): "Laughter"
Ir-Ivah (Ir-*I*-vah): "Overturned"
Ir-Haran (Ir-Ha-*ron*): "Very Dry"
Ka-Dara (Ku-*Da*-ra): "Watcher of Darkness"
Kadira (Ku-*deer*-a): "Set Apart Watcher"
Nura (*Nur*-a): "Light"
Rekém (Ra-*keem*): "Torn Between"
Teion (*Tee*-on): "From the Land of Light"

ΛCKNOωLEδCEMENTS

When an author types "the end" for the first time, the story's really only beginning. Through the immense process of dreaming, plotting, writing, editing, designing, and publishing, I couldn't have done it without a world full of amazing people.

First, dear reader, thank *you*. Either you read this entire novel or skipped to the last page to peek here. It's okay, I do that too. Still, thank you. The fact that you picked up this little story blesses me. Like these characters, I urge you to go enter your world and change it—forever—for the King.

Thank you to the dream-team that inspired me along the way: my family, friends, classmates, and beyond. My sisters— you stayed up till midnight listening to me share every detail, and you were the first to cry, laugh, and chatter about this book. I love you girls! And thank you to Professor Smith for having me write the short story that became this novel. You'll never know how the "Intro to Creative Writing" class changed my life.

To Christopher D. Stewart and the team at S.C. Treehouse LLC: what began as a two-month novel contest turned into this book. I can't thank you enough for urging for me to explore this story! Without that, Érkeos would still be a dreamland stuck in my head.

Every single Alpha and Beta reader including Alea Harper, Anna True, Faith M., Hannah Gridley, Jordy Leigh, Jubilee Faith, Kathryn L., Praise Evangeline, Rachel D., and Sarah Grace Grzy—you girls are the best! Thank you for cheering with me, crying with me, and sharing those fangirling moments that somehow happened. Your advice and encouragement blessed me immensely.

For the interior designing and typesetting: Amanda Tero, you are fantastic! Thank you for being a delight to work with and giving such excellent work.

To Caroline Ruth, my lovely illustrator who endured my demanding questions and quick deadlines while continuing to be such a joy—you're amazing! I always knew your art would be published one day. Now it is!

Alea Harper—wow, girl. I can't thank God enough for bringing you in my life. Your designing skills, editing, suggestions, encouragement. You celebrated with me and helped me through every single rough spot. Alea, you're incredible and my favorite cover designer ever!

Thank you to Misti Konsavage, Aslan Konsavage, and Oma Peterson for their excellent editing services. You guys are the bestest! And I sure hope we got all those commas. Phew.

And to a million other friends who asked, "How's the book going?", volunteered to help, looked at cover art, shared the book with friends, and beyond, thank you. I wish I could say so much more. From blog friends, people on social media, and those I get to personally hug and thank, you have changed my world. I can't imagine life without you.

Lastly, thank You to my dream Giver. God, I love you. Thank You for that first news story about a girl who left home to become a terrorist that I read so long ago. I'll never forget her, because, somehow, she turned into Kadira, and I want to so badly tell her that she's loved, forgiven. Thank You for putting this story in my heart, every single scene that came as I read your Word. And, above all that, thank You for loving me like Father loved Kadira. I don't deserve it. My life is Yours, and I'll seek to keep Your fire burning forever.

// Hosanna Emily

ABOUT THE AUTHOR

Hosanna Emily is an ordinary girl following an extraordinary God. She's a seeker of beauty in the midst of life, whether through creating emotion through ink on paper, dancing under the stars, using sign language in songs, or offering a hug. As a writer, Hosanna wants to showcase the glory of God to the world while reaching out to love others. She published a novella at age thirteen and continues to write stories and share her heart on her blog, Having a Heart Like His. She lives on a farm in the middle of nowhere with her family of 12.

Blog: havingaheartlikehis.blogspot.com
Instagram: @Hosanna.Emily

CPSIA information can be obtained
at www.ICGtesting.com
Printed in the USA
FSHW011443190919
62161FS